The Faith Healer
of Olive Avenue

Also by **MANUEL MUÑOZ**

Zigzagger

The Faith Healer
of Olive Avenue

Manuel Muñoz

ALGONQUIN BOOKS OF CHAPEL HILL 2007

Published by

ALGONQUIN BOOKS OF CHAPEL HILL
Post Office Box 2225
Chapel Hill, North Carolina 27515-2225

a division of
WORKMAN PUBLISHING
225 Varick Street
New York, New York 10014

LIBRARY OF CONGRESS CATALOGING-IN-PUBLICATION
DATA
   Muñoz, Manuel, 1972–
      The faith healer of Olive Avenue / Manuel Muñoz.
         p. cm.
      ISBN-13: 978-1-56512-532-2
      ISBN-10: 1-56512-532-0
         1. Mexican Americans—Fiction.   2. Fresno (Calif.)—Fiction.
   I. Title.
      PS3613.U69F34 2007
      813'.6—dc22   2006031679

10 9 8 7 6 5 4 3 2

To the heart-thieves

and the heartbroken—

our redeemers

and requiters

This, at least, is Real, and what I know.

   —Gwendolyn Brooks, "The Coora Flower"

CONTENTS

The Faith Healer
of Olive Avenue

LINDO Y QUERIDO

PEOPLE KNEW THAT ROAD, that intersection, how often it happens. They recognized it when the newspaper ran a picture from the scene, the motorcycle on the road and a policeman writing something on a notepad. It had been the kind of accident that happens only in fog. But this had been in broad daylight, summertime, the boys coming back from Fresno or wherever they had gone to, and neither of them wearing helmets. At least Isidro made it, people said when they saw it in the papers. The other boy, one of the triplets from over on Gold Street, died right there on the road.

Now look at his mother in that little blue house on Sierra Way with no car out front. Who knows what she is going to do? For days people have been driving slowly past her house. There are no lights on at night, but people know she's there. Perhaps the bedroom where she kept Isidro is in the back, a small lamp providing some light. Like any good mother, she slept in that room, watching him, and when morning arrived, maybe one of her friends came to the house to cook food for the day or to bring groceries. But no. The house remains quiet. You'd never know that poor boy had been in there, the front door closed and never opening.

But it does open, because Isidro's mother must work and get on with her life. Isidro's mother works for a woman on the good side of town, doing work that doesn't need defining. You know what she does and how she does it and how hard it is. His mother knows she is lucky to have this job, because she understands, having lived in the Valley for so many years, that she could be in far worse circumstances. Isidro's mother has no legitimate birth certificate, no piece of paper that validates her name, the day she came into this world, the country she can claim. The woman she works for calls her Connie, because her name is really Concepción and the English way of saying that sounds sacrilegious. That is the name on the birth certificate she has and the Social Security card, too: Connie Islas, no middle name, and not Concepción, but Connie doesn't mind. The documents are fake, cost her fifteen hundred dollars and are for show, to flash at anyone who questions who she is. Thus far the price has been worth it. The woman she works for pays her on the side, a small stack of bills every Friday afternoon, and this has been good enough.

Despite what has happened to her son, Connie sets out from her house on Sierra Way for the walk to the good side of town, in her hand a plastic beach bag that holds her lunch and a container of water. The south side of town has roads so skinny they don't need painted lines; the neighborhood cars must slow down to ease past each other. Her side of town has vacant lots with overgrown grass, houses only sometimes painted, severely pruned trees. She walks past all of this on her way to work, stepping delicately on the worn strips of lawn where the neighbors' grass blends into the street. Connie thinks of her son when she walks past the high school, through the town center with its shops closed because it is not nine yet, past the post office with its flag disturbed by a slight breeze, past the barbershop with the striped pole that swirls all day and night, past the car wash and the gas station, the gradually prettier houses, the greener grass, onto the wide sidewalks and the streets paved rich and dark, to a house with boulders nonchalant on the lawn, a driveway with two cars, and a husband who waves timidly at her as he goes off to his job.

The woman she works for is named Georgia, and every morning she gives Connie a list of things to do, written in English. It is Georgia's way of helping Connie familiarize herself with the language. Connie has worked with Georgia so many years now that the list is no longer just words: *dishes, laundry, dusting*. The house is routine. She knows the windowsills and the closet shelves and the kitchen drawers and the laundry hamper and the husband's habit of leaving socks around and the large potted plants in the foyer and the portraits of Georgia's children and grandchildren on various walls. Connie knows exactly what they own, where the jewelry is, where Georgia keeps her purse and checkbook, what Georgia would notice missing, and thus she has never given herself over to the temptation to take something, something small and easily concealed, valuable at the pawn shops over in Fresno, if she could somehow get a ride there.

This morning, though, is Connie's first day back since the accident. Georgia's house is quiet and the door to the master bedroom is closed. Connie does her morning chores and is surprised to find the house in reasonably neat condition. For a moment, she wonders if Georgia has hired another woman in her absence, but the dusting is so poor that she reasons only Georgia could have attempted it. At lunchtime, Connie takes her plastic beach bag and goes to the backyard. She eats lunch there every day, seated on the little stone bench in the shade or on the deck swing or in the tiny pagoda at the corner of the lawn. Today she wants the comfort of the tiny pagoda.

She can hardly believe it sometimes when she gets to thinking, eating her cold flour tortilla with peanut butter, some summer fruit. She could be worse off: her husband abandoned her when Isidro was seven years old, and women she knows in that same situation have had to move away. But she still lives in the same house because her husband pays the rent and she does not have to say thank you. Isidro's death will not change anything. Georgia and her husband keep her employed, so she has never had to navigate the state services, the scrutiny of her fake documents. She knows she isn't Connie, knows she was not born on July 1, 1955, in Del Rio, Texas, though surely someone was. She's never even been to Texas.

Eating her lunch, she thinks about her parents and how she does not trust them, her parents who shipped her off to a husband when she was very young. Much of what they told her, she knows, was a lie, a confusion. Her father insisted she was born on May 9. Her mother said May 10. Sending her terrible news to them, though, is of no use: a woman used to write letters home for Connie, and when no answers came back, this woman told her that correspondence was often lost in Mexico and never delivered.

Connie has her own way of getting by, and she is not a dumb woman. Plenty of people are in worse spots. Plenty of people cannot sit in backyards like this. What has changed, really? she wonders. Connie knows that people saw her walk along Sierra Way to her job this morning. She knows that people wonder what she does in there, in that little blue house, now that she is alone.

There must be, she thinks, a few neighbors for whom the situation is unbearably sad. Neighbors who cannot believe that anyone would want to be this alone, could endure so many days of being without anyone, no immediate family coming to help. Surely they want to knock on her door after she has come home from work, to ask her if there is something they can do for her, to ask if she wants to sit out on the front steps and just think aloud, talk some. Deep inside, though, Connie knows she would refuse.

She drinks water from her container and notices movement in

the house. Georgia is out of her bedroom and in the kitchen. Her shadow eases across the curtains. Connie imagines the people on Sierra Way looking out of their own kitchens at her house. She imagines them wanting to alleviate the terrible feeling they have about her being alone in the blue house. They go to her front door, knowing Connie cannot be home, and they knock. They knock on the door and stare at the yellow curtains with the eyelet lace trim and the black doorknob chipped at the top, exposing a wink of white plaster. It is a front door with a wide glass plate set hastily into its frame: Connie can remember the green gray putty pressed into place and the fingerprint whorls when the job was done. The curtain moves a little from a fan she has left running in the living room. The eyelet lace trim sways slightly, stops, sways again. But it is daytime and there is no one in the house.

Georgia has done little to intrude, so when she peeks through the kitchen curtains and their eyes meet across the backyard, Connie feels guilty for having caught her. Georgia will step out here now, away from whatever comfort she took sealed up in the master bedroom.

Georgia's husband provides. Georgia has so much, she gives to Connie the things she has no use for. From time to time, they will sort through the bedroom closets and pick out the clothing that will go to the Salvation Army. Georgia is a short, squat woman with legs that remind Connie of the thick tables she dusts in the living room. Georgia's elegant pantsuits and dresses would do her no good, but sometimes Georgia will hold up an item and ask Connie if she wants it.

Oh, the things Georgia has given to her: a practically new color television set, thirteen inches; a Betamax VCR; a winter coat every two years; rain jackets; the plastic beach bag for her to carry lunch; vinyl records of Crystal Gayle and Loretta Lynn, which Connie didn't understand because of the English, but which she listened to anyway because the women's pictures reminded her of Yolanda del Rio, her favorite; an older set of dinnerware after too many pieces had been broken, with teacups and plates that line Connie's kitchen cabinet even though she never uses them; dress shirts and ties that Georgia's husband never wears to work anymore, all for Isidro to have grown into; towels after the fluff has been lost, better to give to Connie than to let her husband use them to dry the car after washing it.

Her prized possession, though, is the bed set that Georgia gave her three years ago. It has held up very well, the Egyptian cotton, "Eight hundred count," Georgia had told her. "Or something like that. Do you know what that is? Thread count?" The set was a creamy beige that didn't look as cool and inviting as it did in Georgia's house. Her own bed was smaller and she could not use the fitted sheet. But Connie cherished the bed set, washing it by bucket in the backyard with a little Woolite and then hanging it up on the laundry line, stepping back with pride to watch the cloth sway in the breeze.

But pride can be an enormous, crushing weight. Connie felt that pride when she was all alone in the house and Isidro soiled his bed for the first time—the weight of her son, how long it took her to steer his body in order to remove his bedsheets. The words of the Spanish-speaking hospital staff came back to her relentlessly in the hour it took to complete the task. *There are ways to pay for his care. Just fill out the applications. We'll help you with the questions you don't understand.* Connie had considered it, but papers paralyzed her.

Isidro had been born in this country on March 22, 1973, and that was his Social Security number on all the hospital forms, but Connie had given none of her own information, for fear the state might take him away. The Spanish-speaking hospital staff assured her that it was not possible, but Connie refused to sign any more papers. She began to cry her refusals, begging them to just let her take her son home. She pleaded with the staff in Spanish to be honest with her — to tell her if her son was going to die, because if he was, then he should be at home.

What the Spanish-speaking hospital staff had given her: plastic bags with liquid inside and a tube to poke into her son's arms; diapers with sticky light blue tape; a large bottle of lotion to rub on his body because Isidro had been involuntarily scratching himself so hard that he broke the skin; ointment for the stitches on his head, and large bandages for the incision cutting through his once-smooth chest; a schedule to tell her when a county nurse would come to make sure the boy was not suffering unnecessarily, a nurse who carried needles and vials with something inside that could erase the pain in her son.

No one in the neighborhood can know how much she suffered being alone with him. Look at the struggle she had removing the soiled bedsheets from underneath her son, and the dilemma she faced down in finally deciding to use her prized Egyptian cotton sheets because there was nothing else.

The nurse came every day for three days, and each day she used more of the vials and the needles, inspected the hard bruises, changed the dressings, checked Isidro's temperature, writing all of these things down in her chart. The nurse spoke Spanish — a large woman in her forties, a little older than Connie — and she spent part of the time trying to convince Connie that it would be best for the boy to be back in the hospital. She showed Connie the forms she had already seen, and Connie held them importantly, but she did nothing with them.

"Bueno," the nurse told her on the second day when the forms were still unsigned and she checked the wounds again. She asked if anyone in the family had come to help her, and Connie said yes.

"Bueno," the nurse told her when she was set to leave and had recorded Isidro in her chart. "While you're sleeping and someone else is looking after him, tell them to watch for the scratching. Use the lotion and try to keep his hands still. He'll want to scratch and scratch and scratch because the blood is slowing down."

Connie sat at his bedside with only a little lamp on and waited. She cried and then wondered if Isidro could hear her. She apologized to him for crying and for not being able to take care of him. She apologized to him for God's allowing this to happen, and said to him that he would have every right to ask God about it when he got to heaven. She sat on the bed and held his hands, felt the veins on his arms, fat from so many needles, his skin too cool.

Connie leaned into him to feel his breath, and it came, belated, but it was there. She straightened out the Egyptian cotton sheets as best she could, and in the morning she washed the other soiled bedsheet and hung it up.

She had fallen asleep, and a knock at the door surprised her. Connie walked to the living room and drew back the curtain on her front door. It was the mother of the other boy from the accident, crying, her two remaining triplets by her side. Connie could only nod her head through her own tears as they spoke on the front steps. She had never met this woman or the boy who had died, but she sensed that this woman knew she had no family, and when that thought crossed her mind, standing and hugging the other mother, the two remaining triplets silent, Connie hugged her harder and then told the woman that Isidro was resting, and maybe she could visit another day when he was feeling better.

After they went away, Connie realized that she had given the impression that her son was home to get better, and she wanted to go after them, to tell the mother that they would soon have equal losses, to say something like *our sons* or *both of them* or *our boys*, but it was too late and she did not know where they lived.

When his scratching began in earnest, the hours slowed and Connie found it much harder to calm Isidro. She smoothed on the lotion, but he kept scratching. He let out deep breaths and groans. The nurse came and went. This went on for hours, from late afternoon till past the time Connie should have turned on the lamp. She did not turn on the lamp because she did not want to see. Isidro's heavy breathing was different — it wasn't a sigh of rest or exhaustion. She knew what was coming. "M'ijo," she said to him, holding his hands, but still she did not turn on the lamp. He could not resist her, she knew, but who was she to hold back his hands? She wanted to let him scratch, to let him at the itch of his own body.

She looks at her own hands now, folded in her lap. Connie is finished with lunch, and without looking at her watch she knows it is near the end of her hour. But she does not rise. She knows Georgia must finally speak to her face-to-face and offer condolence. If she goes inside, she will set about wiping down the kitchen counters or dusting some of the heavy drapes in the living room, keeping busy rather than looking Georgia in the eye. She knows Georgia will come out to the pagoda, so she waits.

Connie sighs. It is true what they say about the last breath. It is so deep and the exhalation is not exhalation at all, but release, with nothing back in. Connie knew what it was and turned on the light. She cried at the unanswered letters that had been sent to her parents. She cried at her husband's having left her. She cried for the bad stroke of luck both her son and that other boy and his mother had had, and then she cried because she could not go to that woman's house to share the misery.

Connie remembers how she said Isidro's name and asked him to forgive her. She wiped at her face and then went next door to use the phone. Connie knocked on the neighbor's door. It was evening and she looked at the street, how the day had passed. A young girl looked at her from behind the curtain, and Connie recalls hearing the girl's father ask her who it was, but the young girl did not answer. The young girl kept staring at her, and the father, fed up with the silence, came over and opened the door.

It is past one o'clock when Connie finally looks at her watch, a tiny silver face with a black band given to her by Georgia. All it needed, Georgia had told her, was a new battery. She sees Georgia coming her way, folding her arms across her bosom even though it is so hot out. Georgia steps timidly toward her bench, and Connie figures this is how you walk toward someone with a great sadness, looking down at the grass.

"You sure you don't want to take the rest of the day off, Connie?" Georgia asks, still standing.

"No," she answers. "I have a lot to do."

"Do you mind if I sit?" Georgia asks, and Connie nods because it is her house. Georgia sits with her arms still crossed, and Connie can see the shoes she is wearing, aqua pumps with a thick heel that must have left small dents in the lawn when she crossed over.

"I'm worried about you, Connie," Georgia tells her. "Charlie and I are very worried about you."

"I'm fine," Connie says.

"Don't you need help? How are you doing it?" Georgia begins, but then cannot say any more. She brings her hand up to her mouth as if to stop herself, and her voice cracks at the end as if she will cry, but Connie can see that the tears are not coming. "You need family," Georgia tells her.

"Yes," Connie agrees.

"Do you go to church? To San Pedro?"

Connie shakes her head and is ashamed to admit it. Such a thing is no one's business, but now that Isidro is gone, she knows what the question implies. How will she bury him?

"Charlie and I were thinking . . . not knowing if you were going to have a service for him . . . if maybe you wanted to have our church perform something. Charlie can talk to our pastor. Only if you want."

A breeze shudders a few leaves in the tall trees of the backyard, and Connie looks up to them. She imagines the inside of Georgia's church, the cavernous, beautiful halls that she sees on very early Sunday morning television. A coffin would look so minuscule in such a place.

"I think it would be a beautiful service. We'd do it for you, Connie. We have a children's choir and I've heard them sing some beautiful songs. 'Take Me to the Water.' Do you know that one? Or 'Shall We Gather at the River'—those songs." Georgia hums a little, but it is nothing Connie has ever heard. "Oh, Connie, those songs always make me cry. 'Jesus, Remember Me When You Come into Your Kingdom.' Oh, yes, that one, that song." Georgia is crying full now. The single hand over her mouth has become two, her fingers covering up her eyes. "It just breaks my heart, all of this, Connie. Just breaks it."

Connie allows Georgia to cry and is too embarrassed to ask her to stop. It has been so long since she has been to a funeral, Connie thinks as she waits for Georgia to finish her tears, but she remembers how people want to make themselves the center of it, to distinguish themselves as the person suffering most. She tries to picture Georgia at the cemetery and knows already that people will gossip about her employer—she cannot allow Georgia to arrange the music.

"I have many things to do," Connie tells her finally, and Georgia wipes at her tears and stands with her. Gathering her plastic beach bag and her container, she steps across the grass, Georgia still with her arms folded. The small dents from Georgia's aqua pumps are there just as she suspected.

"Why don't you come to the grocery store with me and then I'll drop you off home?" Georgia suggests. "These chores can wait until tomorrow." In her aqua pumps, she is going somewhere else, but Connie does not ask where; she only agrees. Though she wants the time to think on her walk back to her neighborhood, it would be good to spend time with Georgia, even if they talk about nothing at all.

On the way to the store, Georgia is careful behind the wheel and they say nothing. At the store, she follows behind Georgia as she fills the cart with more things than she and her husband need, and in the checkout line they both try to ignore the town paper with its picture of the accident. She is surprised, too, when Georgia takes her back to the neighborhood without asking for directions.

"If you need anything," Georgia says as Connie opens the door, "just call me."

"Okay," Connie says. "Good night," she says, as she always does at the end of the day. Once inside the house, she realizes it is only three thirty. She leaves the front door open and turns on the television, parts the curtains in the living room. She is grateful for the noise, but she ignores the television program and watches her neighborhood, where things go on as usual. By nine o'clock, when the other houses have settled down for the night, Connie goes to bed.

Connie wakes up the next morning as if she were going to Georgia's house, but calls her instead. Today she needs to stay home. Georgia's voice on the other end is understanding, but Connie can hear her distress: did she offend her yesterday?

Connie stands in Isidro's bedroom and looks at his clothes. She thinks of scenes in the movies when women collapse like dolls against closed doors while clutching a jacket or a shirt, wiping their tears and looking dejectedly at something in the corner of whatever room they happened to be in. Jackets and shirts, she can understand, but Connie is thinking of socks, underwear, old worn-out jeans that she couldn't give away if she tried. And the other things in Isidro's room, the pictures of basketball stars that he had torn from magazines, toys he had long forgotten. She would have to draw a line, reminding herself that nostalgia had only as much power as she gave it.

She takes down the curtains that cover the sole window in Isidro's bedroom, the yellow curtains that she had put up even though he had protested. Connie sets them to soak in the kitchen sink with a little Woolite. She sweeps the thin rug with a broom and bends down to pick up the stubborn balls of hair. From the single dresser with the broken knobs, the one she bought for fifteen dollars from the next-door neighbor, Connie removes almost

the same items as her husband's from years ago: cologne, deodor-
ant, loose change, hair gel, a bottle of lotion. Isidro had a small
stack of papers from school, his writing in pencil and a teacher's
marks in green ink. Lots of green ink — praise or warning, she
cannot tell which. Near the foot of his bed are his schoolbooks,
with papers tucked in between. She bends down to pick up one
of the books. Math with numbers in complicated configurations
and lots of smiling teenagers with calculators and sharp pencils.
A thick book with four pictures on the cover: a red frog, a desert
landscape, ocean waves breaking, a field of flowers.

Connie had disposed of her husband's belongings slowly and
discreetly. She would bundle a shirt or a pair of pants and take
it with her on the way to Georgia's. Bit by bit, she deposited the
remains of her husband's wardrobe in the large metal Salvation
Army bin, the one right next to the newspaper recycling shack
that sat on no one's property. It took only a few months to clean
him out, draining the cologne out of the bottles shaped like wild
stallions and then tossing away the heavy glass, counting out the
coins she found at the bottoms of some drawers, using some of
his old white T-shirts to wipe clean her windowsills and the thick
pane on the front door.

Methodically, she picks clean Isidro's dresser with the broken
knobs, folds what she can donate anonymously to the Salvation
Army, wipes away the dust. The drawers sound hollow when she
closes them, and Connie slides them back and forth just to hear
that sound.

On the bed is the Egyptian bed set. Even though she washed

and scrubbed at the small dot in the center of the bedsheet, the stain from Isidro is still there. She can still see its faint, irregular reminder. For a moment, she wonders if she should fold the sheets and stack them along with the clothes she will give away, but Connie runs her fingers on the cloth. It is soft as skin, and with the open breeze coming through the window, the fabric feels cool to her fingers' touch.

These are her things. These belong to her. They are worth the effort to save them.

In Isidro's room, she struggles with the mattress, raising it so she can drag it into the hallway and pound it for dust and hair, and then she sees the envelopes. Connie stands there with the mattress lifted, surprised but not surprised. The mattress becomes too heavy to hold, so Connie lets it down. She reaches underneath the mattress—the envelopes are within arm's length, and she pictures Isidro on hands and knees getting them.

Years ago, when Isidro was a young boy, she had seen *Coal Miner's Daughter* on television and cried when the singer silenced her audience by breaking down onstage. Connie had watched the movie on a Saturday afternoon, having recognized the songs from the vinyl records Georgia had given her. Even though she had not understood half of what the characters were saying, she knew the movie concerned a real-life person and gave a complete account of what that woman's life was really about. She saw something in the fans who wanted to pull the singer's hair, a packed house of husbands and wives witnessing their own inexpressible torments about marriage and love and wanting and mistakes. Connie had wanted to sing to an audience like that; she had wanted to collapse like that singer on a stage to earn honest sympathy. She had gone to the bathroom and fluffed a pretend dress and held a hair dryer in an attempt to sing something the way that woman had. She had cradled the extension cord as if it came from a real microphone, but no words had come out, because just as she was about to imitate the English, she had seen Isidro in the mirror, peeking at her through the partially open door.

Connie had stood absolutely still, afraid to move, afraid to draw her son's attention. His face disappeared and the moment fluttered away; she gave the bathroom door a gentle push and closed it shut, then put the hair dryer down as softly as she could. She looked at herself in the mirror. For a moment, she wondered how that actress did it, how she lost herself in that kind of imagination, and if she ever felt ashamed when people watched her act like that.

On her knees, Connie feels that shame now, as if Isidro is again watching her. Within arm's reach, the letters are so easy to clutch, but she cannot pull them out. She knows they are things she should not look at, even if she could read and understand them. She knows that her son must have known, way back then when he was so young, that there were things he should not look at, even if he could understand them.

Her husband had kept three magazines, and one was clearly more loved than the other two.

Connie brings the letters to light and counts them. Nine envelopes, none of them stamped, but all of them have her son's name written on them and nothing else. She sits on the bare mattress and searches for the thickest letter, three sheets of notebook paper folded over, the ragged edges from the wire-bound notebook carefully plucked away. *Isidro*, she reads, and then the date, and then the words start, the words that can give her no meaning, but she thinks she knows enough of them. The closing, *Love, Carlos,* says more than anything else.

Carlos was the boy driving the motorcycle.

As if to make sure, she opens another letter, searching for the openings and closings, and when that boy's name appears again, Connie puts the letter down and sighs. She wonders about the mother of that boy, and she wonders if she knows about these letters.

Everyone knows that road, that intersection. They had been traveling south and had not made the turn east toward town. Connie knows that road: it winds down from Avocado Lake, a place Connie visited many times when her husband was not yet her husband. Up there, the deep green water rushed icy from the tops of the Sierra Nevada. Up there were the picnic tables where families gathered on weekends, and the snaky trails that disappeared into the hillsides. She had been up there — how long you could walk on those trails and never see anyone, then stop and listen to the water still roaring from so far away. As long as that sound was nearby, it was impossible to get lost, the trails so divided and hidden you could do anything up there under the blue skies and not be seen. She remembers those days when her husband was not yet her husband, when she rested her head on his bare chest under the blue skies without being afraid. She remembers what it was like to be so young that she did not recognize that deep pause and heaviness in his chest, the difficulty in saying something he did not want to say. "Te quiero," he had whispered, and she had ignored his hesitation, how he had summoned the words like a hard breath.

For a good part of an hour, Connie does nothing but sit in Isidro's room, looking at the empty dresser, and she realizes that finally grief is coming and she will be washed over by it. She would say, if the mother of that boy came back, that she is stricken with a double loss. Connie stares at the letters, and for the first time she feels a gratitude at her inability to understand this language, the intimacies that surely lie on those pages. She begins to weep and puts her head in her hands, and when she tires of that, Connie takes the letters and begins to rip them into tiny, tiny pieces. Everything, the envelopes, the sheets of notebook paper. Through her swollen eyes, she does her best not to look at them as more than sheets of paper, as meaningless to her as the green ink corrections from Isidro's teacher. But the difficulty, the impossibility, of ignoring the pencil hearts scrawled across the pages.

She rips the letters angrily, just as she did her husband's magazines all those years ago. If her husband had stayed, they would have had a better rein on their boy, and he would not have been on the back of that motorcycle in the first place. She would not be alone in this house as she is, with the pile of letter scraps on the mattress, scraps she will wet in the sink and squish tightly into the garbage.

When they had left Avocado Lake, Connie had sidled up next to her not-yet husband as he drove the way home, her feet curled under her as she stretched the length of the bench seat. Those were the days, when they had a car with a long bench seat, when you could go up to Avocado Lake with no one being any the wiser about what you did up there.

For the rest of the afternoon, Connie works with a new determination; she clears off the magazine pages from the walls of her son's room, folds away the rest of his clothes, pushes the loose hangers to one end of the closet, dusts every corner. She allows herself no time to ponder what she finds in a box of his old toys. Everything she finds, she vows to herself, will go.

Not everything. The Egyptian bedsheet will never lose that spot in the center, but she will get it to fade enough so that someone would have to look very closely to see it. But no one will ever see it. She will sleep on its cool fabric in her own room, in her own house, paid for by Isidro's father, José Antonio Islas of Del Rio, Texas. She will never tell him that his son died at seventeen, and he will continue to sign checks for which Connie never has to say thank you.

They had been coming back from Avocado Lake and they had been only a few miles from town. They had taken the back roads home, through and past Minkler and Reedley. They had only a few miles to drive back to town and the road was so quiet, but somehow sleep would not come. How could it when you were resting your head against the shoulder of the man you loved and you had nothing to watch but the yellow lines in the middle of the road?

The house will be empty, only Connie, only her things. She will become the woman who lives alone in that little blue house on Sierra Way with no car out front. In next week's paper, photographs of her son and the other boy will appear: Isidro Islas and Carlos Martínez, handsome in their school yearbook pictures. The day of the first funeral, a line of cars will drive through the town, out toward the cemetery near the foothills. Mostly kids from the high school will come, because neither family has a lot of family. Isidro's funeral will be the second one, but Connie and the other mother will attend both. Connie will be unable to say anything to the other mother at the first funeral, and that very night she will wonder if she should make a gesture of friendship to her. But at Isidro's funeral, it is only the same: the mother and her two remaining triplets in the same clothes, Georgia crying just as much, and a group of high school girls huddled together and trembling in their tears. "Un Puño de Tierra" will be the song that moves everyone to tears on both days, even those who don't understand it. Sorrow, after all, comes in so many languages.

Those high school girls will forget him. People will not remember.

Connie will dream of the boys on a motorcycle. She will dream of her son hugging Carlos as the motorcycle speeds faster. This was love. At each of the intersections, she is there watching as

Isidro hugs Carlos, feeling with her son as Carlos takes in a deep breath, the boys waiting for clearance, Carlos's back widening. Isidro could not have known how men sigh with a deep pause and a heaviness, why they sigh like that. Isidro hugging him because this was love and there was so much of it ahead for them, so much.

Up in her closet's top shelf will sit her son's wallet, its battered leather, handed to her by the police at the hospital, and a Giants baseball cap. Connie will regret having destroyed the letters: such beautiful things, even if she did not know what they said. If they had been her love letters, she would have written *lindo y querido* to say it all: beautiful and dear, lovely and loved. But she never sees that kind of sentiment anymore except in the old bars of Fresno, scripted on the neon beer signs lighting a map of Mexico.

Such beautiful things — they were the only things, really, worth keeping. Connie will wake up in the middle of the night and stare at the dark space of that top shelf. It will nag at her that the cap might have belonged to the other boy, and that there is another mother in town just like her.

BRING BRANG BRUNG

LINCOLN SCHOOL, ON THE north side of town, on the good side, without a single railroad track in sight, is where Martín enrolled Adán for kindergarten. When Martín was growing up, Lincoln was the rich-kid school and, by default, better. When his mother drove the back way home from Thrifty's after an ice cream cone, you could see how much bigger the Lincoln playing fields were, and the blacktops still without the basketball nets ripped down. Nowadays, Martín wasn't so sure how good the school was, but when he moved back to the Valley from San Francisco, he looked to rent first on this side of town, even though the places were too big for just him and Adán. There was Roosevelt School over on the west side in a newly incorporated part of town, brand-new buildings and landscaped fields resurrected from abandoned orchards. Or Grand View, where all the farmers' kids went, a tiny school a few miles out of town, springing up out of the grape vineyards, teachers always yelling at the children during recess when they cornered a gopher snake and threw rocks at it. Wilson and Jefferson he crossed out immediately, both of them on the south side of town, where he had grown up — on Gold Street — and now home mostly to kids struggling with two languages. It hadn't been so bad when he was young, but later, when he was in high school, he would drive by those schools and wonder about their disrepair, their inadequacy, the ponds accumulating at the bus stops during rainstorms, the kids haphazardly jumping across them, trying not to get their shoes wet. But he settled on Lincoln because he remembered how that part of town had clean streets and sidewalks and wide lawns. There was never mud on that side of town, never a flooded street or a sewage leak. The north side was pristine.

At the school's front office, painted in the same clinical, soothing light green he remembered from Jefferson, Martín held Adán's hand. The boy quietly watched as Martín set down the pile of identifications: Adán's birth certificate, his inoculation records, his preschool report cards. It took him a moment to recognize the woman at the desk, who had smiled wanly at him when he entered, unsure of how to approach him: she turned out to be Candi Leal, a girl he'd gone to high school with and a good friend of his younger sister, Perla. He had never liked Perla's friends, a whole brood of mean, belligerent girls whose troublemaking began with skipping school and ended with pregnancies by the tenth grade, the father-boys nowhere to be found. But here was Candi, who had had her own kid, if Martín recalled correctly, sometime in the eighth grade, and now she was a grown woman in a respectable job at the very elementary school she had attended.

When he stated his business, without really saying hello to her, Candi slid him some forms and a pen, glancing down at Adán, who stood on the other side of the counter as if waiting for questions. Martín ignored her, deliberate in writing out the usual information: child's name, parental contact information, emergency phone numbers. He pressed hard through the triplicate, lifting the sheets just to check if the marks had gone down all the way to the goldenrod at the bottom. When he got to the section about Adán's mother, Martín casually slashed a large *X* across it.

"So when did you move back?" Candi asked. Her tone wasn't innocent and it wasn't oblivious: Martín knew she had already heard from Perla.

"Last month," he answered as Candi skipped her fingers down the information on the forms.

"San Francisco's tough," she said. "Expensive, too." She reached the section he had slashed out and paused, looking at it for a moment, as if she expected to learn something.

"How's your kid?" Martín asked her. "He must be in junior high by now."

"Eighth grade," Candi replied, but she didn't say anything

more. She gave Martín his goldenrod copy and told him when Adán should report to school. He tried to get her to look him in the eye the whole time, knowing he had the upper hand, the way people would be prying and wanting to know. People had made their mistakes a long time ago, when they were young and hadn't known better, and he was perfectly willing to remind them if it came to that.

ON THE SCHOOL DOCUMENTS where Candi stopped her fingers, in the space slashed out in pen, was the story: the small town just south of Orlando, Florida, and a burial in the torrid heat, tropical humidity searing through Martín's suit. Missing from that document was a name — Adrian — and a sudden aneurysm late at night in an airport hotel room in Denver, Colorado, during a business trip, and a family in Florida who had barely acknowledged Martín and offered no comfort. What Candi wanted to know, when she asked Perla, was more about who Adrian was and what had happened, but Perla had no way of knowing about any of it. Martín had kept Adrian close and offered little; not even Adrian's death would change that. No one but he would know about the uncomfortable trip to Orlando for the funeral, or about the cousin, Priscilla, who was cordial, but whose cowed silence, in the end, meant Martín would have no ally in Adrian's greater family. No one — not even Adán, who was too young to be able to remember it fully later — would know about the cheap, pink-walled motel room where they had spent the night, a heavy breakfast of eggs and hash browns the next morning before the flight back to San Francisco, Martín staring out the taxi window at the pastel colors of Florida, knowing he would never see it again. If Perla had been with him, maybe her defensive, angry way of seeing the world would have prepared him for the legalities and the long, fruitless contesting of beneficiary money. Perla would have said he hadn't fought hard enough, that you get only what you fight for, and whatever he lost to Adrian's family was the result of his own stupidity. Perla would have said this if she had known the whole story — but it was almost as if she knew the undercurrent of it when Martín announced that he had to move away from San Francisco and come back to the Valley. "Is that right?" she had said, over the telephone, her voice coming over, he thought, with barely disguised triumph. "You can stay with us if you have to," she had offered, meaning with her and her now-teenage son, but Martín had politely refused.

Before long, though, it was humbling to face what was happening with his finances and, for once, to admit that circumstances could overwhelm a person. Always, Martín had been a person who believed that choices governed your road: you had to look past the crumbling downtown and imagine something better. You had to count the pregnant teenage girls and swear not to get involved in anything like that. You had to think of the orange groves nestled on the brink of the foothills and look past the deep green leaves for the meth labs hidden there. The Valley was a mess of lack, of descending into dust, of utter failure, and he had learned that long, long ago. But in the San Francisco apartment, opening the letters from the Florida lawyers and reading the documents that allowed Adrian's family to siphon away what little had been left behind, Martín finally came face-to-face with failing. He thought of the helplessness of his sister when she had her baby, the decisions she had to make as a teenager. He thought of other girls like her, sitting in family courts, in lawyers' offices, at juvenile detention centers where the father-boys served out a month or two. He thought of the cruelty of Adrian's family, saying nothing about wanting to gain custody of Adán for themselves and bring him to Florida. In the end, he was the same as those girls in retreating back to the Valley. He would have to make do.

In his honesty with himself, Martín would never call himself arrogant, but he knows Perla would. And she would call him hypocritical, insensitive, unforgiving, judgmental, quick tempered, and mean spirited. She could very well have reveled in his struggle. Still, on the day he had made the move to the new place in his old hometown, Martín had finished the long trip from San Francisco with Adán sleeping the entire way, and there was Perla on the sidewalk. She knocked on the passenger window, waking Adán, and waved a stuffed purple elephant at him in greeting. Adán had rolled down the window, smiling for the first time in many weeks as Martín parked the car.

"Look what your aunt Pearl has for you," she said to Adán. As for Martín, she greeted him cautiously, a hug that felt more like letting go.

IN THE LATE-DARK of the new house, in the rooms that echoed with their emptiness, by the wide windows that still had no curtains and let in the streetlight, Martín was the one who could not sleep for nights on end. Grief would come like a ghost at the foot of the bed, just as he was sleeping, and the curve of Adrian's face would ask why he was trying to forget.

He ignored the grief as best he could and fretted endlessly over the new circumstances, trying not to toss in bed, because Adán slept soundly next to him. Despite having his own room, Adán refused to sleep alone—this the only indication in his behavior that something was amiss. In the first few days in town, with Martín not yet prepared to look for a job and running daily errands to get their house in order, Adán had fidgeted and scrambled in every line Martín had to wait in. If Adán wasn't playing with another child in line, he distracted himself with the simplest of things: a pebble in an empty plastic bottle, a nickel deposited over and over into a pay phone. Misbehavior, if Martín correctly read the reactions of the faces around him, but he paid them no mind. All the better to exhaust Adán and not have to battle with him at bedtime, leaving Martín the night hours to go over what needed to be done.

In the dark, he owned up to how he felt about Adán: this was not his child. All along, it had been Adrian's idea; it had been Adrian who had spoken plainly and honestly with a woman he'd been friends with for years—Holly, a chubby white girl from way back when in Orlando. Martín had gone along with the idea, perhaps not fully grasping the responsibility but assured by Adrian's enthusiasm. Adrian would be the one to raise him, and he would be the one earning the money, too: a sales job took him up all around the western states, commissions rolling in, Martín maybe too self-satisfied with a no-nonsense accounting job he had in Oakland. The mistake was colossal. He had never considered what it would require to be the child's sole guardian. In the dark, he had to raise himself quietly from the bed, careful not to wake up Adán, and pace in the kitchen, wondering how he would ever admit something like this to Perla.

What plagued him most was the repetition, the continuation of a cycle he had thought he would never be part of. One afternoon in town, stopping at the post office to mail off documents to yet another lawyer in Florida, Martín had caught a glimpse of Perla's son, Matthew. He hadn't seen Matthew except in pictures, and even those were of his nephew when he was nine or ten. Martín knew it was him, though, because he looked every bit like the skinny white boy who was his father, a troublemaker who disappeared long before Perla even knew she was pregnant. Martín had gone to school with that guy, a year ahead of him; he still remembered his slouch, his dirty-blond hair, the way his eyes always looked bruised and damaged underneath. His nephew looked enough like that guy for Martín to do a double take, and that's when the sadness of the situation hit him deeply. His nephew was fifteen, a walking mirror of his absent father, the same darkness under his eyes, and it was all Martín had to see to understand why Perla never brought him over to the house.

To be in a house with only one parent: look how it had turned out for Perla. Their mother had fought with her repeatedly, pointing to her older brother as an example. Of course, Martín had deliberately set an impossible standard, out of sheer distaste for his sister's belligerence, her selfishness, her disrespect, and her stupidity. He went to church even though he didn't like it, just to have one more thing over her. Perla fought against rules, leaving the house in the middle of the night, sometimes letting the car that came to pick her up idle shamelessly right in front of the house, just to wake up their mother. Such rebellion — it scared Martín now, alone, even though the prospect was years away with Adán.

In the dark of the kitchen, sitting at the kitchen table, which had only two chairs, he poured himself a glass of milk. He would never dare ask Perla to discuss their mother, how she truly felt about her. They did not speak to each other. But surely Perla knew that their mother had also stopped speaking to him after he moved in with Adrian. Both of her children, then, were cut off: a monumental anger she had with them for having failed her.

This is how he thought at night, starting with simple, solvable problems like the electricity bill or a doctor's appointment. Grief summoned itself, impossible to release, Adrian insisting himself back to life — Martín had to ignore it to keep from being overwhelmed. Then a wave of guilt would sweep over him for his inability to completely summon a love for either Adán or his sister. Eyes open in the dark, he would sit in the kitchen until sunrise, asking himself questions that were impossible to answer. What would make him happy, satisfied? How would his mother have answered that question? Perla? Had their mother favored him more because he looked like her and Perla looked like their father? Did Matthew know that he looked like his father and that Perla saw it every time she looked at him? Is it possible to will yourself to love someone? If it isn't love, then what is it?

BY THE BEGINNING OF October, with Adán a few weeks into kindergarten, everything eased some when Martín found a job at a small accounting office in Fresno. The job wasn't the best of circumstances: the building was on the south side, the more dangerous part of the city after dark, and the office was situated in a converted warehouse, the false ceiling perfect for tossing up sharpened pencils to see if they would stick. Drafts of the hot afternoon air somehow snaked past the warehouse's corrugated paneling and into the core offices, which were nothing more than walls of Sheetrock; in the mornings, the drafts were chilly enough to force Martín to drink a third cup of coffee. Every Friday afternoon, the secretary would come around with the paychecks, personally signed by the company owner, and Martín would not complain about the ten minutes he'd be docked if he had been late.

Perla mercifully made it easy for him. She kept her phone calls cautious and intermittent, but when he told her that he had found a job, she had been the one to volunteer to care for Adán after school. "I'll pick him up and bring him to your house or mine, whichever," she said. What, then, was she doing for work? Martín wanted to know, especially with a teenager at home, but he felt too ashamed to pry when he himself was in need. "My house," he had told her, and gave her a set of keys.

Most days, after he came home from work, Perla wouldn't linger more than a few minutes before she excused herself, touching Adán gently on the shoulder. Neither Martín nor Perla would bring up the subject of money, but it was on Martín's mind once a few paychecks came his way. He knew taking care of Adán was costing her something, and he knew her willingness to help was rooted in a desire to move past their differences. Somewhere along the line, like her friend Candi Leal at the front office of the elementary school, she had eased into a forgiveness of the world at large, and that included him. One Friday night, he came home to find Perla cutting up a roast chicken from the grocery store and Adán busy folding paper towels for the table. "I bought dinner," she said. "I hope you don't mind. Matthew fends for himself most times anyway." In helping her set the table, Martín took a peek at the receipt in the bag to see how much she had laid out for everything, the containers of macaroni salad and wild rice, the rolls. She had bought beer, too, but that would be for later apparently. When they were ready to eat, he insisted she take one of the two chairs, and he ate leaning against the kitchen counter.

When bedtime came for Adán, Perla helped get him into pajamas and cajoled him into sleeping in his own room. "Here," she said to him, handing him the purple elephant. "Me and your dad will be in the kitchen, so no monsters can come, okay?" Martín, putting away the dishes they had washed, could hear the murmur of protest, but Perla's voice was gentle in its command and patience. "I'll leave the door open a little bit, but be a big boy and go to sleep," she said, and made her way down the hallway to the kitchen.

She pulled two cans of beer from the refrigerator and handed him one. "I went to the school today," she said, sitting at the table.

"Yeah? Why?"

"The school pictures they took the first week? The money? A kid in the fourth grade took the check you gave him."

"That was weeks ago," he said, thinking of the morning he had given in to Adán's pestering to wear his favorite sweatshirt—a purple one with a green dragon on it. "I forgot all about it. He never said anything."

"Did you expect him to?" She took the tiniest sip of beer from the can, licking her lips a little, and it occurred to Martín that he had never actually seen her drink before. She was almost demure about it, and it reminded him of one of the first times he'd gone out to dinner with Adrian, to a restaurant with thick tablecloths, and of the careful way he'd had to handle the wineglasses. He tried to picture his sister at such a place.

"He got beat up that day," Perla added. "Or shoved around. You know how kids exaggerate a little. I don't think he really got hurt."

"Who was the kid?"

"Just some older boy. Probably the older brother of some kid in his class."

He took a deep drink from the can. The beer was watery and cheap, but he said nothing because it was from Perla's courtesy and generosity. "You should have called me. I would've come down and taken care of it."

"What was there to take care of? You can't be bothered at work right now. Not with you just starting and everything. I know how bosses can be."

"So what did they do? Did they punish the kid?"

"Well, the principal—do you remember Roberta Beltrán? She was three years ahead of you, or something like that. That really fat girl? She's the principal there, if you can believe it, and she had that boy in tears in no time. He still has the check, and he has to bring it to the school on Monday."

"For what?"

"To apologize. He's supposed to write a letter." She laughed, shaking her head. "Can you believe it? That's the punishment. We would've gotten a lot worse back in the day."

He laughed with her, but it felt forced. He took another drink of his beer, noticed Perla looking down at the lip of the can as if she had remembered suddenly what it had been like for her as a teenager, as if she had become lost in pinpointing where the trouble had started, how young she had actually been.

"You know, I hate to ask you, but I gave them some of the money for the pictures. I told them you'd bring the rest on Monday."

"Oh, yeah?" he said, putting down his beer. He reached into his back pocket for his wallet.

"I had twelve dollars on me. So you owe them thirteen," she said, getting up from the chair. She went into the living room and reached behind the couch, where she had hidden the pictures. "I wanted to bring them to you as a surprise, so you wouldn't have to wait till Monday."

He pulled a twenty from his wallet, this being payday. Then he pulled two more and put the bills on the table as Perla made her way back.

"It was just twelve, Martín."

"Yeah, I know, but you've been doing a lot for me. It's just a little bit." He reached for the pictures and pretended to study them closely. Only the head of the green dragon on Adán's sweatshirt was visible, a cartoon dragon with bubble eyes and a little tongue upturned as if in thought or effort. Adán was smiling in the photograph, as if nothing had happened that particular day. All the pictures were the same, but Martín slid them out for inspection so Perla could reach to the table and fold the bills quietly in her hand.

"Who does he look like?" she asked Martín as he returned the pictures to the envelope.

"More and more like his father," he nodded. "Adrian was Cuban. Dark hair, a little wavy," he said. "Dark eyes."

"He's kind of light skinned."

"His mother was white. A friend of Adrian's." Perla had never seen a picture of Adrian, and he thought for a moment that she might ask. He didn't know whether he would show her or, if he did, where he would begin the story. Maybe from the beginning, which was the end. When he moved into the new place, he had left pictures of Adrian packed in their boxes, hoping Adán wouldn't say anything about them.

Perla went to the refrigerator to get another beer, and she turned to wiggle a can at him in invitation. He nodded and she brought them back, popping hers open with relish and taking a longer drink this time. "In the car," she said, "on the way home . . . he told me that he looked like you."

Martín almost snorted and ran his fingers through his hair. "Oh, Jesus," he said, sighing. "The things I'm going to have to explain to that kid . . ."

"Well, you know, I'm here to help you," Perla said, tapping her fingernails nervously against her beer can. "You're my brother."

"Yeah," he agreed, but couldn't add much more. Part of him felt ashamed at Perla's attempt to bring their slow reconciliation out in the open, felt ashamed of how little he was trying to meet her halfway.

"I've learned a lot trying to raise Matthew," she said. "I made a lot of stupid mistakes. So did some of my friends, the ones who had their own kids. It's hard, Martín. It's harder than you think."

He looked at the picture of Adán, the joyful color of his purple sweatshirt and the cartoon dragon, and found it hard to imagine a point when Adán would fully form into his own person. The fourth-grade boy couldn't have been more than ten years old, and already he had discovered that you could bully your way through this world if you wanted. You didn't have to follow the rules.

"Perla," he asked, "what do you do for work? For money?"

"I clean houses," she replied. "Mostly here, but sometimes over in Reedley or in Visalia. A lot in Visalia. There's people moving there from the Bay Area. Lot of money."

"Not me."

She laughed slightly. "Normal situations, I mean. People who had money to throw around to begin with, so they buy land and build these really huge houses to live in, and then rent tiny apartments in San Francisco so they have that when they need it."

"Is it enough? The money you make?"

She sighed and put her chin in her hand. Her hair was pulled back and knotted up almost haphazardly, and though it was as long and black as he remembered it, the sheen was a little dull, as if her hair were somehow thinking of shading gray. It was hair pulled back out of necessity, to keep it out of the way as she hurried in the morning, not like she wore it in high school — combed razor-straight like the other girls', her eyeliner heavy, and her lips glossy with a deep blackberry. "Money comes and goes," Perla said. "I work hard only for myself now. I used to do for Matthew, used to do a lot, but he's just a real angry kid. He's got a lot inside him that I can't get to."

"He looks like his father. That kid — "

"Well," she interrupted, "that's the problem, I think. Every time he looks in the mirror . . . the things he says to me sometimes." When she put her hand to her mouth, the way she did that, he thought of their mother and her regretting. "I'm almost thirty years old, you know? I did what I could and the rest is up to him. If he wants to come home, well, then he comes home. And if he stays at a friend's house, that's none of my business anymore. You can't control that if they don't want to let you."

When she began crying, as he expected her to, Martín sat quietly and watched his younger sister's resolve shimmer through the helplessness. One hand was still on the beer can, and because he looked closely now, because he paid attention, he saw that she wore no nail polish, and the two rings on her fingers were simple, unadorned silver. Rings she must have picked out for herself, shopping alone at one of the malls in Visalia, studying the velvet display boxes intently, not bothering to worry over the price, thinking of herself for once. But it wasn't selfishness — Martín understood that. It wasn't like the way he thought of himself, of deserving and wanting, the self-satisfaction and the near greed of having, after years of not-having. Instead, it was a contentment and a self-knowledge, a forgiveness for her own part in her unhappiness, a releasing.

"Do you want another beer?" he asked her. "Finish off the pack?"

"I have to drive home," Perla said, dabbing at her eyes gently.

"Sleep on the couch," he told her. When she didn't answer, he crossed to the refrigerator and brought back the last two cans. Perla popped hers open as if with effort, grinning a little, and before she took a drink, she raised her beer as if in toast. They tapped cans, the aluminum sounding as sincere as glass.

MONDAY MORNING, HE CALLED in sick to work, and though the secretary quizzed him, Martín held his resolve over the phone and promised to be better by the next day. The principal had asked to see him at ten o'clock, and he arrived at Lincoln School fifteen minutes early. Candi Leal, busy with the phones and a string of kids slumped in plastic chairs against the wall, nodded knowingly at him, raising her wrist to tap at her watch: she'd get to him soon. On the way there, Martín had imagined himself speaking to Candi at her desk, prompting an exchange that he should have engaged in weeks ago when he had registered Adán. She was too busy now, and he regretted how he might have misread her before, her initial spark of forgiveness, of new possibilities, of growing and maturing, and how he had wiped it away by not returning her grace.

Almost on the dot, the door to the principal's office opened and Roberta Beltrán came over to shake his hand. "Good morning," she said good naturedly. "It's nice to see you again." If anything, she had gained more weight; she had always been a large girl, but now her size gave her a commanding presence Martín had always associated with both principals and mean teachers. "Jesse," she said, crooking a finger at a boy in a Raiders jacket. "In my office, please," she ordered, then turned to hold the door for them.

"We'll make this quick," Roberta said, sitting at her desk and clasping her hands. "Jesse, do you have something for Mr. Grijalva, like I asked you on Friday?"

"Yes," Jesse answered in a half groan as he dug into the pockets of his Raiders jacket.

"Sit up straight, please," Roberta ordered as Jesse took his time finding a piece of paper that he then unfolded. "Speak clearly."

Jesse read from the paper, his voice flat footed despite his sincerity. "Dear Mister Grijalva, I am sorry that I stole the money from Adam and that I brang the money to my house. I am sorry that Adam did not get his pictures because of me and I am sorry that I hurt his feelings. Sincerely, Jesse Leal." Finished, he handed the letter to Martín.

"And where is the check?" asked Roberta.

Jesse fished in the jacket's other pocket and drew out the check, folded tiny in a triangular shape, its edges smoothed down and worn.

"Unfold it," Roberta said. "Is that how you took it from Adán?"

"No," he answered. His fingers seemed confused by the folds, but he unraveled the check and smoothed it against his leg before handing it to Martín.

"Thank you," Martín said, taking it.

"What do we say?"

Jesse turned to her, confused, but Roberta only tilted her head down at him, as if looking over the brim of a pair of glasses. "We need to apologize."

"But I did . . . ," he protested.

"You read the letter. You also need to say it like you mean it. Look him in the eye."

Jesse Leal turned to look at Martín, and though he said he was sorry, he drawled it. Martín nodded his head as if in acceptance, but he thought of the battle Jesse Leal would turn into, a ten-year-old who had somehow already managed to persuade his parents to buy him an expensive Raiders jacket. "Fine," he said to Jesse Leal. "Just don't do it again."

"You're excused," Roberta said, and Jesse turned abruptly to the door. "Get a pass from Ms. Leal to get back to your room," she called out after him.

When the door closed, Martín reached for his wallet and pulled out the money he still owed for the pictures. "Was it twelve or thirteen?"

"Thirteen, I think. But Candi knows for sure. Why don't you give the money to her?"

"Okay," he said, but before he walked to the door, he asked Roberta quietly, "That wasn't her kid, right? Candi's?"

Roberta shook her head and reached for the phone. "Oh no," she said, dialing. "Maybe a cousin of some kind, but not her kid. She had her own problems long ago." She waved good-bye to him as she waited for her call to go through.

SINCE HE HAD THE rest of the day off, Martín went to the Kmart in town. It had opened when he was in high school, but now it was losing out to some of the newer chains at the broadened strip mall. He found a large frame for Adán's picture and then bought a smaller one to give to Perla.

Waiting in line to buy them, he pulled out the check and the handwritten letter from Jesse Leal. When Jesse had read it, there had been no way to imagine how lousy every aspect of the note would actually be: the lone, emphatic period, circled dark and certain when there were clearly two sentences. The misspelling of every name except his own. The crabbed penmanship. Martín bristled at the blatant *brang*. He thought of Roberta Beltrán and Candi Leal and any of the people he had grown up with who might be teachers now, of all of their night training at the local colleges, their effort to push books and paper in front of kids like

Jesse Leal. Somewhere along the line, they would know when the right time had come to correct these errors, before they became bad habits, more obvious in speech: these were the smallest of a whole string of corrections, and Martín multiplied them by the numbers of kids in the office this morning, of the kids waiting in the classrooms, the enormity of the task. Perla had failed. His mother had failed: he remembered that day when he was a teenager, when he had opened the envelope from the adult-training center, the application that his mother had put in, the handwriting scratchy and uncertain, the information inaccurate or missing because his mother had not understood the questions. Her application for job training had been denied. He had thrown it away before she even saw it. Diction, syntax, grammar, basic math, conceptual thinking. Symmetries, the logic of sympathy, the order of gratitude, empathy, concern, the rigor of understanding, the faulty equation of grief and anger. He had failed, too, somewhere along the line. He handed the money for the picture frames to the woman at the register, her bare arms thick and dark, her red smock rumpled from a long early morning shift. He thanked her aloud when she handed him his change.

At the house, he put Adán's picture in the large frame and hung it in the living room. For a brief moment, Martín considered putting it in the hallway, just as his mother had done in their house on Gold Street when he and Perla were growing up. Their individual year-by-year school pictures, Perla in her glasses and barrettes until she changed into the girl with the razor-straight hair in eighth grade. Pictures of him and Perla when they were both very young, their mother with them, standing behind proudly, and even a picture with all of them: Martín, Perla, their mother, their father, the photograph so old that the tint had washed out in an odd red hue. But the living room it would be, just Adán's photograph above the couch. There would be time enough for others.

Later, he left a message at Perla's inviting her to come for dinner, and after he picked up Adán from kindergarten, they went to the grocery store, where Adán helped select the dinner items for his aunt Pearl. He let Adán call her whatever he wanted and didn't correct him. Though he had no reason to be, Martín felt exhausted, but there was dinner to make. There were many days ahead. Still, when they got back to the house and before he started dinner, he fished in one of the boxes that he had stashed away in his own bedroom and found a picture of himself and Adrian. He loosened it from the layers and layers of plastic he had wrapped around it, Adrian coming back to light. His mother, upset, would say she could feel a knot in her throat, but the Spanish word meant more: *un nudo* — and then the gesture toward the neck as if to ward off the noose doing the damage. Martín gave the frame a quick swipe with the hem of his shirt and set it on a little table in the living room.

ON THE DAY OF Adrian's plane trip to Denver, the morning had brought a hard rain to San Francisco. The two of them had shuffled quietly around the apartment, packing Adrian's suitcase. Adrian would return on Monday night if there were no delays — Denver meant the possibility of snow. Adán slept with a raging fever, and for a rare time, it would be Martín taking complete care of him. There would be no driving to the airport, no good-byes with tickets in hand.

That rainy morning, the apartment sat dark. The windows let in a weak light. Adán didn't budge in his sleep, though his face was flushed and his pajama top soaked through with sweat. There was a sticky pink medicine that smelled like citrus.

Martín spent all day in Adán's room with the apartment quiet. He spent the day looking out the window at Coit Tower in the distance and fell into a well of doubt. Adrian was a good man, but he was all his own and not fully Martín's to love. There was a young child here, but he was Adrian's, not his. After years of wishing for a relationship, here it was, but with it came a certain boredom and an isolation. Martín found himself longing for something to change in his life. He thought, for the first time in years, of his father, and in the quiet of the apartment, Martín let himself inch toward understanding him.

Adán's fever broke that afternoon, but he remained sleeping. The daylight stayed the same gray—it was impossible to guess the hour. Martín flipped through four magazines and tried to read a book, until finally the call came from the Denver airport, Adrian's tired voice telling him that he had landed safely. Martín wasn't up for much talk; he wanted to go back to the warm, quiet room of just thinking, of solitude, so they chatted for a minute at most. Monday would come soon enough.

All day it rained. Nothing changed. It rained all day.

THE HEART FINDS ITS
OWN CONCLUSION

THERE WAS MORE TO it than a woman with long black hair, flipped high in front, a woman wearing just pink panties low on the hip, her hands on a sheer curtain, a woman looking out of a window, down into the street. Cecilia wished she could remember the face of the man who had just left the room, who had closed the door after himself, and the woman who had put her hand against it as if the door had captured his warmth. But that had been years ago, back when Cecilia was a child, and the actress with the long black hair had never become famous. That woman couldn't be easily found and identified. She wasn't

Mia Farrow with her shorn hair in *Rosemary's Baby*. She wasn't Jane Fonda with her voice crackling ominously over the radio from North Vietnam. The film, too, had been forgettable: a drug-running movie from the 1970s, set somewhere in a dusty outpost in Mexico. Cecilia remembered nothing of it beyond glimpses: the cars like the woman's hair — long and black — with windows tinted against the sun; men with guns shooting for the glory of the sound; a fat man being lifted away from a room, a squealer who had faced his punishment, his white shirt bloody and open, showing the full expanse of his belly; the cars giving chase to one another, careering past potholes and kicking up dust, bouncing and jostling like their old family car. But the story, the how of that woman. What she saw when she looked out of the window of the dank, tiny room with an even tinier bed, a bed she had shared passionately with the man who had just left her. Cecilia didn't remember that: that had been where Tía Sara had covered her eyes, tsk-tsked between her teeth. A dank, tiny room with a single washbasin jutting out of the wall, a mirror over it where the woman could have washed her face and looked up at herself to discover her own longing. That, though, Cecilia only invented. There was nothing but a room, a departed man, and a woman in pink panties with long black hair.

Over there was the Crest Theater — the cine — its once grand, sparkly marquee where Tío Nico and Tía Sara took them to see movies. The marquee stood bare now, the lights off. Those years ago, the cine had been no place for children, but there they had been, Cecilia and her cousin Sergio being herded toward the flashing neon. Cecilia had held on to Tío Nico's hand as the woman behind the small ticket booth spoke into the speaker box. The booth stood at the edge of the cine's facade, the marquee twinkling bright against the long, sloping entrance to the doors. Her booth shone warm and bright, with room enough just for her stool, and she slipped tickets through the mouse hole in the glass. Cecilia still remembered all of it: the shiny tiles of the cine entrance; the click-click of Tía Sara's high heels as she edged to the doors, then the quiet carpet once they got inside; the aguas frescas bubbling in their fountains; the Mexican candy with a scarlet rose on the wrapper; the tall stacks of paper cups, swirled in purple and green; the length of the lobby and the ladies waiting patiently outside the bathroom door; the slender wooden phone booths and a man getting inside one, sliding the door against the crowd, a light turning on so he could see; the smell of sauerkraut and mustard and jalapeños from the side counter; the whirr of the ice cream machine; the door to one of the theaters opening and tinny voices coming through like caught conversation.

She could see the cine from where she was parked, close to the front doors of the bus station in Fresno. She'd driven a long way to pick up her cousin Sergio, who had called her at work late in the afternoon. Since her desk at the insurance office was right next to her boss's front door, Cecilia had urged Sergio off the phone with a quick approval, even though getting to Fresno meant at least half an hour of driving. When the six o'clock bus from Bakersfield arrived, Sergio hadn't been on it.

It was February and dark by six o'clock. There, on the south side of Fresno, on the fringe of downtown that emptied after dark, there wasn't much except vacant parking lots and very dark spaces. Cecilia was frightened of Fresno these days, how Fresno had gotten to be like this, all big-city trouble and worry. Every day in the break room at work, Cecilia read the newspaper, and there was always some terrible story coming out of the city. Clerks being shot in gas station holdups; teenage boys getting guns from who knows where. She knew danger, the difference between accidental and deliberate harm, the difference between the trouble in the city and the tragedies of everyday life in towns as small as hers. At the insurance office, Cecilia filed all the initial slips for the month's claims and witnessed the peril in everything. A house fire in Selma; an old man who slipped in the tub, now on his way to a rest home in Parlier; a school beating more brutal than usual in Visalia; car wrecks all along the too-thin roads dissecting the county; farm machinery accidents she wished she had never read about. A despondent farmer who had come in to tell about a group of kids with matches sending his barn up in flames and his having to race down and shoot one of his badly burned hogs to put it out of its misery.

"I really have to get out of here," Sergio had said, and Cecilia heard what sounded like desperation. "I'm going whether you help me or not, Cecilia, so come get me. Please."

Sergio lived with her tía Sara in Bakersfield, and this was what bad blood meant: Cecilia was now twenty-three years old, and she had been raised by Tío Nico and Tía Sara after her own parents were killed in a train accident in Mexico. Bad blood meant that when Tío Nico and Tía Sara divorced, Tía Sara took Sergio to Bakersfield to raise their son under strict religion. Tío Nico kept Cecilia because she was his brother's daughter, and blood meant something to him. Both sides had done their best to turn the two cousins against each other, but Cecilia had always known better. To help Sergio, she would have to lie to Tío Nico, but that was fine—the problems he had with Tía Sara were between the two of them.

How bad it had to be for Sergio to leave, Cecilia didn't know, even though he should have moved out and gotten a job when he graduated from high school, two years ago. How bad it had to be for his voice to shake with worry when he called her, Cecilia couldn't say. She had heard his voice catching over the phone. She had never heard him sound like that before, and it was enough to bring her here.

Cecilia could hear Highway 99 off in the distance, even with the windows sealed up. Its presence was all around downtown Fresno: on-ramps and off-ramps, the road signs that glared bright with reflection, the stark stretch of overpasses and the starker worlds underneath them. The six o'clock bus, empty now, departed along a side street. Three taxis lined up to take away the few standing passengers. The station stood quiet once again. Cecilia could see the clerk behind the long desk, dressed in his blue uniform and hat, reading the paper, and she watched him for a little bit, hoping he would reach for the phone or the radio to hear about another bus coming late. But he was as still as the empty streets around the station.

Nearby were the new county offices where Tío Nico cleaned. He told Cecilia that he left promptly at five o'clock during winter because the downtown area was so dangerous. He would be dismayed if he knew that she was here, waiting for Sergio. *Bueno pa' nada*, she could hear Tío Nico say about his own son. *Not worth a damn thing, and he's a drain on you. He knows you've got a job and that's all he cares about.* It was difficult sometimes for Cecilia to reconcile that Tío Nico was talking about his own child—though they were cousins, she could not think of Sergio as anything but a brother. But then again, Sergio was difficult: he called his own father Tío Nico. Cecilia could never refuse her cousin. She wasn't at all like her aunt or uncle, before or after they separated.

She tapped her fingers on the steering wheel, impatient. The station clerk nodded off behind the glass. Evening was just beginning, but in this part of Fresno, with its quiet streets, the hour seemed deep into the night, the buildings around her glimmering half-heartedly. A taxi prowled by but, seeing no one on the sidewalk, sped off in the direction of the train station, which was newer and better lit.

In the old days, before the new train station, the buses brought everyone in. Cecilia remembered clearly the amount of traffic around the bus station on the nights they went to the Crest. All those years past, the adults so careful in spite of the brightness of the neon, the packed parking lot and the families milling about, the long line snaking away from the ticket booth. The buses delivered wave after wave of workers from Los Angeles and San Diego. Barbershops and shoe stores waited over in the Fulton

Mall with doors open and inviting, just walking distance away. There the men, if they had the money, suited up in cowboy hats and new Wrangler jeans, and in the theater, the smell of their new haircuts gently wafted down the dark aisles. Back then, things were grander. Cecilia didn't know how those men made a living, how they managed to find a place to stay; she knew only that they showed up in nicely pressed shirts and held open the doors for the ladies every chance they had. Now, only danger surrounded the parking lots with their cracked asphalt, potholes, muddy patches, and sagging fences, all the lights gone dark.

A car was coming down the street, rolling slowly, and Cecilia could see the driver scanning the sidewalk. It was a black car, something from the late eighties, a Cutlass maybe, if she remembered correctly from filing so many insurance claims. The car was coming in her direction, slowing down even more, and she did her best not to look at the driver. But she couldn't help herself, the driver having rolled down his window to the cold February night air, and when the car passed, Cecilia looked over and the man behind the wheel stared back.

Her heart raced. Those forms she filed, those stories she read. You give the teenage boys the money they want. You don't ever go to a service station after nine o'clock. You don't let the kid ride with you on the jumpy seat of a tractor, no matter how slow it's going. You look in every direction before you enter the intersection, and you let the rain and fog slow you down. Yet here was the car turning around and pulling up right behind her, the headlights on and the man's silhouette rigid in the driver's seat.

He idled the engine for only a moment before he turned it off, and his headlights went out as well, making the inside of Cecilia's car seem a deeper dark than it had been before.

She put her hand on the ignition and waited. Over in that bus station, she could see the clerk still nodding in sleep. Her heart raced, raced as it had in the days of the Crest cine, just over there, where the woman with the long black hair had stood at the window, her hands lovingly stroking the curtain, when a knock at the door made her turn around. The woman had walked over, the sound of high heels amplified — yes, only panties and high heels. The hoots started from the men in the back row. The woman had opened the door, and two men immediately forced their way into the room, demanding to know where her lover had gone. The whistles from the back row grew fiercer still, Tía Sara's tsk-tsk ever sharper as her thick hand tried to shield Cecilia's eyes. But Tía Sara had been just as engrossed in the story as the men in the back row, and she had been concerned for this woman in the face of menace. Her aunt's thick hand had loosened, and Cecilia saw the two thugs begin to rough up the woman. The men had whistled louder as the woman screamed her denials. Cecilia remembered her gigantic, round breasts, the deep swollen purple of the nipples, the way the thugs brushed their hands against them. Cecilia had wanted love to come back into the room, for the woman's man to return and save her. Her heart had raced and raced, set in its own belief that any moment the man would come back.

Cecilia heard the car door open and saw the man step out.

She watched as he nonchalantly began his walk to the station, his footsteps echoing against the sidewalk. Cecilia leaned in, ready to press the horn full force just in case. As he passed her car, he leaned down a bit to look inside and caught her glance.

"Hey," he shouted so he could be heard through the window, "you his sister?"

She turned the ignition.

"Hey!" the man shouted. "Hey!" He jumped in front of her car and tapped hard on the hood. "You his sister? Are you Sergio's sister?"

Cecilia had not turned on the headlights, so she could not see his face clearly. Through his winter coat, his shoulders stretched powerfully and explained his fearlessness, his hands still on the hood and him standing right in front of her car.

"You don't need to be scared of me," he said, shaking his head. "I came for your brother." He lifted his hands from the hood, as if in surrender, and pointed to the bus station. "In there? You want to come in there?"

He began walking toward the station, where the clerk was still asleep. He walked toward it but still faced her, waving her in his direction, encouraging. The sound of his footsteps receded, a fainter clicking against the sidewalk, and it reminded her of the woman in the movie and her high heels, how the sound wasn't matching exactly with the precision of her steps. Cecilia lost herself watching the man get closer and closer to the door — he was wearing boots, some kind of dark shoes with a heel, and his winter coat reached past his waist. The lobby gleamed in its fluorescent light, promising safety: she could rattle on the clerk's window if she had to.

She turned off the ignition and gathered herself. Her keys in a tight fist, purse crooked in her elbow, Cecilia stepped out of the car. She crossed her arms against the cold and half ran to the door, keeping her eyes fixed on the clerk behind the glass. The lonely drone of Highway 99, off in the distance, filtered through the empty parking lots and into the streets, the wire fences slouched and creaking. She rushed even faster as she got closer to the door, almost running inside, the doors banging heavily back into place, the sound echoing in the empty lobby. The clerk, though, made no motion. He still slept, his face obscured behind the cloudy partition to his booth, the thick pane scratched with large gashes.

The man was sitting on one of the orange plastic benches. He had taken off his coat, and Cecilia could see now that he was powerful, his shoulders massive and round. He was older than her, older than Sergio, maybe in his late twenties but she couldn't tell for sure. He sat leaning forward, elbows on his knees and arms extended, legs spread wide, claiming space. She caught the glimmer of a thin gold chain around his neck, his hands clean of rings, hair cropped so short the scalp showed, a goatee busy around his chin. She hadn't noticed that in the dark.

"So you're his sister," he said.

She didn't move. "I'm his cousin, not his sister."

"Well, that's what he told me," the man said.

The clerk finally stirred in the booth and, seeing someone

standing in front of the partition, sighed heavily and sat up straight.

"Cecilia, right?" he asked, but when she wouldn't answer, he rolled his eyes. "What? Are you a Bible-thumper like your mom? That woman rags on me something hard. Do I look like a bad guy to you?"

"Yeah, I'm Cecilia," she said. She felt caught, having to admit this. He was talking about Tía Sara; he had somehow been at the house in Bakersfield. She turned slowly to the station doors as if to check for the next bus, but it was embarrassment and nerves and shame that made her want to turn away from this man. She didn't know how to ask him who he was.

He seemed to know. "Sergio ever mention me?" He waited for her to speak. "Huh? Sergio ever mention me?"

Through the doors, her car seemed farther away than she thought. On one of the opposite corners, Cecilia glimpsed a woman waiting to cross the street, hand on her hip. The woman was wearing a short skirt and heels, impervious to the cold, heading in the direction of the old Chinatown a few blocks over, where all the prostitutes congregated. Cecilia scanned the horizon, looked over at the Crest, its dark arch barely visible.

"He has something of mine," the man said.

With that, she turned to look at him. "Who are you?" she finally demanded. "Sergio called *me* to come pick him up, not you."

"You don't know me?" His voice pitched higher, edging toward frustration, maybe anger. "You don't know who I am?"

"No," she finally said. "I don't."

"He's got my heart," the man said, melodramatically holding his hands across his chest, but he sneered a bit when he said it. "He's got a lot of things I want back."

Cecilia stared at him, his goatee, a way of sitting that had grown into an arrogant posture, the size of his shoulders, and his shorn head. She could picture this man laughing at Tía Sara. She wanted to speak sharply to him, but she knew she would have Tía Sara's voice—powerless, no matter what the anger and vehemence. Tía Sara's voice, back when they were children, fell up against Tío Nico's louder, more vociferous yelling and drowned in his heaviness. Tío Nico's voice was like the men who had cat-called in the darkness of the Crest cine, right over there, all of the men in the back row with their newly shined shoes and slicked-back hair, their voices rising to a slur of cheer and whistle, so loud it was impossible to hear what the woman with long black hair had wanted to say in protest. The woman had wanted the two thugs at the door to go away, to stop harassing her, but the men in the theater somehow urged them on.

"You look just like him, Cecilia," the man said to her, and she remembered then how Sergio's voice had shaken with worry on the phone. "He's a pretty little bitch."

"Jesus . . . ," she muttered. Because of the empty street, she knocked on the clerk's booth, rapped her knuckles on the scratched partition as if he were still sleeping. "When's the next bus?" she demanded.

The clerk was about Sergio's age, dark skinned and gangly, with a head of thick, uncombed hair. When he stood up, she could see that his uniform shirt was too big for him and that he wasn't wearing a belt. His pants drooped down past his hips. He reached over impatiently for a clipboard, eyeing Cecilia.

"The seven o'clock," he told her. He had a little speaker vent in the partition like the one in the booth at the Crest. "It stops in Goshen and Tulare before this."

"Is it going to be late?"

"Schedule says seven o'clock."

"That's not what I asked you," Cecilia told him gruffly. "Is it going to be late?"

"They're on time."

"Can you radio or something?"

"Nah, I can't." She could tell he was lying, but it wasn't worth the trouble to argue with him. The clerk deserved none of her nervous anger, none of her confusion as she struggled to come up with the reason behind Sergio's phone call, his fleeing, and now this man sitting in the bus lobby waiting for him.

"You want to follow me to Goshen?" the man asked her. She heard him stand up, his boots sounding against the lobby floor, the footfalls slow and patient and coming toward her.

Cecilia didn't want to answer him anymore. She didn't want to speak another word to him, but she could do nothing but wait and stare outside again, standing by the doors of the bus station. The man's footsteps came closer and closer, and when they stopped, she didn't have to turn around to know that he was there, behind her. She folded her arms against herself, against the anticipation of having him touch her.

"Suit yourself, then," the man said, and he brushed past her, pushed himself through the lobby doors and into the night air. He stood on the sidewalk, facing the street and not turning around.

By the station clock, the next bus would be arriving shortly. There would be no time to race down to Goshen, a little town with nothing but a bus station closed after dark, a little town darker and quieter than this part of Fresno. Sergio would not think to get off in Goshen. If he had seen her car there, he might have gotten off, glad to see his cousin, and Cecilia cursed herself for not having thought of it sooner. But there had been no way of knowing. There had been only Sergio's voice and the passing, fleeting sigh she had made on the phone, her resignation at his supposed despair. There might have been worry in his voice, but Cecilia's imagination had led her no further than Tía Sara's open Bible, her old hands steadying on a choice line. There had been no way of knowing, of preparing for possibilities, of finding a way to prevent consequences. If only Sergio had mentioned this man waiting out on the sidewalk, then maybe she could have gone home and pleaded with Tío Nico to come to Fresno with her, because strange men were always dangerous.

Over along the wall was a bank of telephones, and Cecilia searched in her coat for coins. She shook her purse, hoping to hear the tiny scatter of loose change, but there was nothing or not enough, so she dialed the operator and gave the woman the number to Tía Sara's house in Bakersfield.

"Tía, it's me, Celi," she said loudly, as if the operator were deliberately taking her time, and then her aunt's voice came over the line, timid in its confusion.

"Celi? Celi?"

"Tía, I'm at the bus station in Fresno. Sergio told me to come get him." She turned to look outside, where the man was still standing on the sidewalk, his large hands jammed impatiently in his coat pockets.

"Ay, Dios mio, Sergio," her aunt said. "Celi, bring my son back here to me."

"Tía, there's a man here waiting for him."

"Ay," she said again, but this time it came as a near sob, as something said with her hand on her forehead, the anguish overcoming her so much that she couldn't say any more.

"Tía, please. Who is he?"

"He's been running with a bad crowd, m'ija. I don't know what Sergio has gotten himself into these days, why he's like this. That man is terrible. He's the devil . . . "

Cecilia had to pull the receiver away from her ear, laying it close to the top of her shoulder and closing her eyes, wishing it could be simple: Who was this man, and how did Sergio know him? Why was Sergio running? And why hadn't Tía Sara overcome her lifelong rage and simply called Tío Nico's house, admitted that there was trouble and that she could not handle it herself? Her aunt's voice flowed, incessant, onto her shoulder, but she knew her aunt could tell her nothing.

"Tía," she said, interrupting her, only to realize that Tía Sara had already started sobbing. She listened to her tears over the static in the line. "Tía," she said again, hoping her aunt would collect herself.

"Pray with me," Tía Sara told her, sniffling, and she could almost hear the pages of her old Bible turning in her lap, the big Bible with the red dye across the top. "Please pray with me, pray that Sergio knows this is a house of love."

"He knows that, Tía," she said, sighing. "I'll bring him home."

"Please, Celi. You remember, don't you? From Primer Corintios. Recite with me," she pleaded. "You remember. 'Love is patient . . .'"

"Love is kind," she had to say, because Tía Sara had paused, her tears on the brink of starting again, and Cecilia could not bear to hear them. She knew what was behind them, every time Tía Sara wept like this: the agony of having made the wrong decision years and years ago, having left Tío Nico, having separated the children as they did, the troubles with Sergio only pointing to her failure.

"It always protects," her aunt recited softly. "It always trusts."

Even from the bank of telephones, Cecilia could hear the bus approaching, the chug of its engine from down the street. "It's here," she told her aunt, who was still reciting. "I have to go, Tía. Sergio's here." She hung up the receiver with Tía Sara still in midprayer and rushed over to the doors. The bus had pulled up alongside the curb, its brakes tightening and releasing in a hiss, exhausted. The man inched closer to the front of the bus, waiting for the door to pop open, while behind the bus's tinted windows, silhouettes rose from their seats and gathered in single file to disembark.

The driver got out first, an older man like Tío Nico, his face framed by giant glasses, a graying mustache. He came down lithely, a vigor in his step, and stood at the bus's foothold, his arm extended out at the man who stood waiting for Sergio, as if to bar him from approaching. He was letting the passengers exit, and they came forth in a steady stream — men just like the ones Cecilia had seen years and years ago, still coming, still arriving with nothing on them but a wallet of emergency money. They stepped off one by one, and whenever a woman prepared to descend, the old driver extended his hand graciously to her, then helped the children she was inevitably towing along. The sidewalk gradually became crowded, the passengers pushing back even the man waiting for Sergio. There was luggage in the bins of the bus's underbelly. There were cars coming now, out of nowhere, waiting across the street, people coming out of them and collecting their long-awaited arrivals. There was something disarming about all the activity, such a sudden cacophony of voices, and it made Cecilia feel safe. She stepped out of the lobby to the loud sighing of the bus in idle, of cigarettes being lit in relief, keeping her eyes on the line of silhouettes still on the bus. Taxis pulled up as if summoned, and the cabmen opened their doors and waved people over, crying out, "Anywhere! Anywhere! Five bucks!"

She saw Sergio, her cousin, her brother, step down out of the bus, a grocery sack under his arm. There were clothes in that sack — there had to be. That was how Tía Sara had run off in the initial days, stuffing what she could into a large paper bag and dragging Sergio with her. How ridiculous, Cecilia thought immediately, how it must have signaled that the gesture was nothing but dramatics and flourish. It was all for show, all for presenting to the waiting relative who offered the warm bed: this was all they could take with them, all they had time to bring.

But just as she was about to raise her hand to Sergio and wave him over, to get him in the car and admonish him — just a little bit — for such unnecessary worry, Sergio saw the man waiting for him, and the look on Sergio's face sank into terror. He began to push his way past some of the other passengers, but the man rushed at Sergio and caught him by the shoulder, enveloping him, his face scowling.

"You little fucker — you think I didn't know you'd come here?" The man hit Sergio hard against the back of his head, his palm flat and backed by the force of his rolling shoulders, and Sergio's hands reached up to feel the spot, to ward off another blow. His hands were working on reflex, Cecilia knew, and he let out a shocked grunt that caught the attention of everyone surrounding them. The women with their children brought the little hands closer, not knowing what to do because their luggage was still in the underbelly of the bus. The men did nothing but watch.

"Sergio!" she called out, moving to them, but the man hit him again and Sergio dropped the grocery bag. One of the passengers absently picked it up and held it out to Sergio, as if ignoring what was actually happening.

"Celi," Sergio said, finally seeing her. "Just stay out of it." Tears had started in his eyes, and he took the grocery sack from the passenger who held it out to him. The man grasped him gruffly by the arm, hand gripped right under Sergio's armpit, lifting him past the other passengers, heading toward the black car. Cecilia started after them.

"Didn't you fucking hear him?" the man called back at her. "Stay out of it, you fucking bitch!" he shouted, so loud, as if signaling the men from the bus not to interfere, and they made no motion to help Cecilia.

"Llame a la policía," one of the women whispered, so quiet.

He shoved Sergio into the passenger seat. Cecilia stood looking on, unable to move, and she began to cry, watching Sergio wide eyed in the car, his head hanging down. "Sergio!" she called out, and the same woman spoke up again, her voice more insistent: the police, the police. But it was happening too fast for her. Sergio made no motion to get out of the car and run — to what? — even as the man slammed the passenger door and walked around to the other side. He turned around to glare at her, keeping his eyes unblinking and stern as he started the car, and then he drove off, speeding down the street.

The passengers around Cecilia stared at her indecision. The women with children rushed to get their luggage, looking impatiently for their rides, and Cecilia knew what they were thinking. The escalation of arguments, the return of that man, maybe a gun and shots being fired. Hadn't they all seen stories like that? Hadn't they all witnessed what men could do when love was denied? Hadn't they all recognized a man's way of loving, of loving what he could not have? The men from the bus began to walk away, uninterested, and Cecilia silently cursed them through her tears, cursed how ineffectual they were, how their bravado was held in reserve when it really mattered.

The sidewalk was emptying. The old driver lowered the doors to the luggage bins, gently bringing them back into place. Cecilia watched him because she did not know what else to do. The taxis began to drive away with passengers inside, and some of the people turned to look at her through the back windows as she stood there. The sidewalk would be bare soon, and she knew better than to be standing there alone. There was nothing left to do.

The bus driver came over to her. The wrinkles in his face softened him, as did his gray mustache and thick glasses. Faded and clouded like the panes of the clerk's booth, the plastic lenses were from a state-aid program, Cecilia knew, the frames old and well worn, but the man had been careful with them. He blinked hard at Cecilia, as if he were having difficulty seeing through to her.

"You okay, mujercita?" he asked, blinking at her as if hoping she would say yes.

"I'm fine," she answered.

"They did the same thing in Bakersfield. But that was in the afternoon, so there was a police officer." He kept staring at her, waiting for her to respond, but Cecilia had nothing left to say.

"Thank you," she said absently, for lack of anything else.

"It's not like the old days," the old driver said. "People used to be a lot more civilized. People never acted like this."

He turned and eased up onto the first step of the bus. He finally strained, showing his age, the effects of the long drive. "So sorry," he said, turning briefly, and then he closed the door and started up the bus. He pulled it away and headed down the street, leaving the front of the station quiet again.

She had to go now, before it became late, before the sidewalk was completely bare of people. She would have to tell Tío Nico, find a way to inspire some kind of sympathy for his own son. She would have to ask him to call Tía Sara to find out what they could do. Tía Sara would not cry in front of Tío Nico. Tía Sara would put up a front of resilience, and Cecilia counted on that.

Walking back to the car, holding her keys, she saw the glow of the Crest Theater over in the distance, its neon faint over the empty parking lots. Impossible, Cecilia thought, not after all these years. It could not be. It had to be a church occupying the old dusty seats. It had to be a real estate agency lighting the place in an attempt to promote the building. Not a movie, not even a Spanish-language film these days.

Instead of heading in the direction of the highway, Cecilia drove the other way, toward the theater, just to see, though it would take her deeper into downtown Fresno. The neon shone brighter as she approached it, not one letter unlit in the theater's name, scrawled across the facade. But the booth was empty and dark; there was no one there.

She idled the car at the intersection facing the theater, and she saw herself being led out of the place by Tía Sara those many years ago. She had begun crying in the middle of the movie, at what had happened to the woman with the long black hair. The two thugs had barged into the room, and one of them closed the door. The other had clapped a hand over the woman's mouth when she began to scream. The men in the back of the theater whistled louder, the woman's large nipples purple in close-up, her legs straining to balance on her high heels. The single wash-basin had a purpose then — one of the men turned the faucet, and there was a squeaky rush of water. They shouted questions at her, demanding again to know where her lover had gone, and when she wouldn't answer, the sink full now, the two men grabbed her head, her hand reaching up, as if by instinct, to stop them. As she was bent over the sink, breasts dangling, the backs of her thighs stretched in full view, the men in the theater cheered louder: "¡Eso!" *¡Right there!* "¡Eso!" The two thugs had begun drowning the woman wearing the pink panties, and that was when Cecilia had rushed from her seat and bolted toward the lobby, the doors with the leather padding and small windows of light showing her the way out.

At twenty-three, Cecilia had not seen death personally. It had never made its presence known, not in the flesh, not in the im-mediacy of her everyday life. Her parents' death had come only as news, something told to her many days after it had happened, as cold and clinical as the insurance claims she filed at work. She knew now that she still underestimated the fragility of life, that all (and everything) it meant was absence. But how did she know, back then when she was so young, that absence sprang from the spilling of blood? That absence began with a blow to the head, the rupture of skin, the throated cry, the body moving of its own accord, making some last gesture—it was the last she saw of the woman in the pink panties, her arm uselessly fending off the thugs, the men in the back row still cheering.

The intersection was deserted and Cecilia turned the car, suddenly frightened, suddenly fearful of not making it home. She checked the locks on the doors. Even after the bare spaces of downtown Fresno, she would have to travel thirty miles of dark, lonely roads, once she left the city, before she made it back into the safe arms of Tío Nico, who was still a comfort no matter what he thought of Sergio. Still, she knew, the terrified look in Sergio's eyes belied a choice: he realized what had happened, how his plan had failed. That man without a name had a way of loving, his way of loving what he could not have, and it was not her place to say sorry. Sergio had stayed in the passenger seat, waiting for the man to drive him away, and her heart had to embrace Sergio's decision. It was like that woman's hand, her last desperate gesture: her body refused, gave way only by fighting, but her heart found its own conclusion, and it knew there would be no lover to come back and save it.

Fresno receded into a shimmering line in her rearview mirror. The February night was broken only by her headlights, but all around her were the dark fields where so many terrible things had happened to so many people. She would be home soon, crying into her uncle's shoulder, but now Cecilia wished, somehow, that it would be Tía Sara. Those many years ago, in the grace of the cine's lobby, away from the pain on the screen, Tía Sara had bent down on one knee, bringing her in, holding her against her silk dress and the gentle scent of powder on her neck. The ladies who were lined up to use the bathroom looked on and nodded their heads in sympathy. Cecilia wailed terribly, unable to find enough consolation in Tía Sara's arms. The woman behind the counter came over with a fresh ice cream cone, holding it wrapped in a little paper napkin. The ladies kept looking on; some came over with tissues, with hard candy, their high heels sinking quietly into the carpet, so gentle.

WHEN YOU COME INTO YOUR KINGDOM

DRIVING HIS CAR ON his way to work, windows sealed against the heat that was already building, Santiago remembers the coast. It's easy to remember, here in the dry stretch of the Valley during the summer days, below the sky that isn't as blue as it used to be — such haze — along the length of Highway 99 nearing the interchange to the new 41 and a clog of cars. If you drive south, away from Fresno, toward even flatter, drier country, you'll soon reach the Grapevine or Kettleman City, the escape hatches.

Santiago remembers the coast, thinks of it, its pull and pleasure. He provides: he has taken his family out of the Valley numerous times, past the rush of interior Los Angeles and then over to the coast. He knows very few who can leave for pleasure's sake. Very few who look at travel as necessity, as escape, and he has long stopped trying to convince his co-workers at the warehouse that a weekend away is not really an extravagance. Santiago knows how they think: his co-workers calculate the price of gas, fast-food stops, tickets to Disneyland, parking, some quick way to stop their kids from crying in the gift shops. But that isn't how Santiago provides; that isn't how he treats his family.

Santiago stays away from the theme parks and instead takes his family for a day's stay at a hotel along the coast, that and nothing more. A hotel stretching into the sky, a pool down below with guests lounging, the Pacific close enough to shudder the palm trees. The rules for his two kids are simple: swim or sun or read or listen to music or go back inside the hotel room and watch TV, but never complain of boredom. Hotels — even out-of-the-way hotels — are sanctuaries, full of businesspeople, high heels clicking, rolling suitcases, dark oak doors, elegant restaurants with cloth napkins, elevators with charming bell dings. Years ago, when the kids were much younger, Santiago insisted they fit their toys into their small suitcases, nothing dragging behind them, nothing to upset the order, no crying, no pestering. No matter which hotel they ended up staying in, the ambience was always the same, the travelers — in a sense — always the same, and he wanted nothing to upset that order.

It is summer, deep in July, and in the evenings when he gets home from work, Santiago flips on the television and waits for the weather forecast. Such boredom for the forecaster: always in the hundreds, always the Valley map shown in red, searing like an aching bone deep in the arm of California. Down at the coast, though, the colors are a cooler orange and yellow.

It is summer and it's been months since the coast. February, in fact. This Tuesday morning, on his way to work, while the traffic at the new interchange slows, Santiago is trying to remember. Drivers don't know what to do these days, after so much construction and with so many new ways to get to the other side of Fresno. The traffic stops altogether; he will be late. He thinks of the last hotel they went to, back in February, the tall hotel that nearly kissed the shoreline, the pool deck built next to a small pier, the bobbing of little boats. The room on the eighth floor, the door opening out to a breezeway, and his wife marveling at their luck — an oceanfront view! — the kids hunching over the balcony and pointing at the pool deck, grabbing their towels, and rushing down. Santiago had yelled out to the kids that they would be there soon and not to run, but he had held his wife back from following them and stood with Luisa in the open door of their room — a door with forest green paint and a diamond-shaped placard with the number 806 in brass, lounge chairs placed conveniently outside the door, the walls lemon colored. He kissed his wife, held her for a moment, and she smiled back at him — it had been a very long time since he had seen that look on Luisa's face — and then they gathered their own things to go to the pool.

Santiago remembers that long breezeway, the row of doors on one side, then the wide expanse of the ocean on the other. He remembers thinking that later in the evening, it would be nice to sit with his Luisa on the breezeway and watch the fog roll in, gathering itself together way out in the distance to make its way onshore.

By the time Santiago pulls into the dirt parking lot of the warehouse, there are only two slots left and he's twenty minutes late. Though it's just past seven in the morning, the long rolling doors have already been pulled open and a freight truck sits with its side belly open to a forklift. The school district's work trucks stand side by side on the opposite end of the lot, face-forward, but so far none of them has left for the day. The groundskeeping for the school lasts all year, but summer brings the major overhauls: painting, repairing light fixtures, leaky pipes, and outdoor water fountains, replacing broken windows, waxing floors, fixing lockers. Start time is seven because of the heat, with a half-hour lunch and a quit time of two thirty. From the warehouse doors, he sees Carrasco smoking a cigarette, his clipboard tucked under his armpit.

"Hey, Salinas, another day," Carrasco tells him as he makes his way to the doors. "When are you taking some time off?"

Santiago is surprised that Carrasco isn't upset about the twenty minutes. "Haven't thought about that."

"Maybe a little time away," Carrasco says, looking at him and then down at the clipboard. "Clear your head some."

"Yeah, but . . . you know, money's tight right now."

Carrasco stubs out the cigarette and then leans down to pick up the butt. Even the warehouse environs are part of their regular duties. "Summer's the best time to work. Best time to make money, my dad always said." He checks off a few items on the clipboard. "You're doing doorknobs today. Next two weeks, actually."

"Doorknobs?"

"Superintendent lost the grand master key. Opens every single door in every single school building of the district. So we're cutting new keys and redoing all the doorknobs."

"No shit."

"You got the kid in there cutting keys," he says, waving to the air-conditioned office where one of the high school students logs hours in a summer work program. "I'm teaching him to code the keys. Sure you don't want to take that time off?"

"What a mess," Santiago says before stepping into the warehouse to put away his lunch.

"It better not be," Carrasco tells him. "And don't take the interchange next time. Everybody's been late for the last few days."

In the warehouse, past pallets of cheap paint ready for summer use, the rest of the crew comes in and out of Carrasco's office. Two refrigerators sit in one corner of his office, along with a soda machine. Santiago wonders how Carrasco gets any work done in there. Carrasco's phone keeps ringing because he is hardly at his desk to pick it up. The radio crackles with commands from crews already on the job at some schools, asking for an extra ladder, fresh paintbrushes, longer hoses. Blueprints sit stacked roll on roll on a counter, haphazardly labeled and dated. Fresno State calendars line the walls wherever there is space, sometimes partially covered by beer ads, bikinied women with high heels and big tits, smiling and bending over. In the middle of all of this chaos sit pictures of Carrasco's family: his wife and his three kids, sometimes as a group, sometimes just the kids, but all of them displayed in oversize, ornate silver frames. In one of the pictures, Carrasco wears a button-down shirt and a tie, and only by stopping and looking closely could you tell that the shirt was patterned in tiny, lilac-tinged checks. Santiago never had the nerve to look that closely, but several jokers on the crew didn't mind making an inspection every now and then, just to make fun of how Carrasco's wife dressed him.

Despite the clutter and the clamor of the crewmen dusting up Carrasco's office, Santiago carries a particular envy of the space. Though work can take him anywhere from a gymnasium to the dark upper catwalks of the high school auditorium, he has no place such as this to come back to, no quiet space to sit down in, where he can write out and organize his work reports once he completes a task. Everything is jotted down while he sits in the cab of a work truck or stands in the empty hallway of one of the school buildings, paper up against the wall because he has forgotten his clipboard. Of course, Santiago knows that it is ridiculous to expect that all thirty men on the crew would have their own offices, but nonetheless he wishes he had a comfortable chair, a phone, clutter still organized enough that he'd know where the important things lay hidden. A shelf above a desk to house photos of his family. A day of shopping on the weekend to pick out frames. Something silver with curls cut into the design, like vines climbing a trellis, or maybe just a simple, sleek finish. Something to gleam nicely against an office lamp, the fancy banker's kind with the translucent green shade. Carrasco's authority gives him license to exhibit the privilege of a good job: his wife still pretty in what must be her forties, his three kids smiling through the ease of their lives. They lack nothing.

"Mr. Salinas?"

It is the high school kid, standing in the doorway of Carrasco's office, holding a box. "Mr. Carrasco asked me to give you these for the morning."

"What is it?" he asks him, coming over and peeking into the box. There are neat rows of tiny manila packets on one side and a jumble of brass key chambers on the other, each looped with a small identification tag.

"It's the first set of keys I made," the teenager states proudly. "I've tested them, too, so they should work." He is taller than Santiago by about two inches, and even though he is narrow in the shoulders, Santiago can tell there is another growth spurt coming, more change on the way.

"How old are you?"

"Sixteen."

"Yeah? Sophomore?"

"Yeah," the teenager answers. "Well, I was. I'm a junior in September." He holds out the box to Santiago as if it were suddenly heavy.

"All right, then," Santiago says, taking it. The teenager walks back toward the main office, and Santiago watches. From this angle, all the awkwardness of his youth glares through. The pants are too short, hovering just past his ankles, and if he lives where Santiago thinks he does, the pants will have to last until the end of summer.

As Santiago walks out to the work truck, he thinks of his own kids, his own boy and girl, and the inevitable comparisons spin in his head. The teenager's voice hangs with him—*I'm a junior in September*—the deep register, his Adam's apple knotty. He is a boy progressing solidly past adolescence, and Santiago thinks of his son, Alejandro, but refuses the memory. There is still his daughter, Eva, who has fared well—pretty like her mother, reasonably smart in school, if a little lazy at homework. But better still, she carries a brashness about her that Santiago secretly likes and encourages, however much mouthing off to teachers and students alike gets her into trouble. What it means, Santiago believes, is that his Eva will be no one's fool, and that eclipses all the easy, dumb dreams Santiago used to have of his children being doctors or lawyers. What matters more is temperament, self-sufficiency, persistence, doggedness, self-awareness, the ability to make others feel a little less important than you, even if you have to be mean about it. Look at Carrasco.

No one is at the work truck, so Santiago takes the driver's seat and waits. After a few moments, he turns the ignition and beeps the horn at Carrasco, who still stands at the rolling doors of the warehouse, making a few last scribbles on his clipboard. Carrasco waves him on—a partner will join him later.

Better to be alone this morning. Better to be alone altogether, given how his mind has been working lately, always turning, never letting him rest. Carrasco knows — he needs the vacation. He needs the drive down to the coast, the waves approaching and never ceasing. He needs to get away from the heat, the tired wake at five in the morning to make it here on time with the summer hours. He needs to get away from sitting on the edge of the bed at that early hour, wondering how he can go on, how people go on when the speck of doubt turns into a weight too massive to ignore, where everything from Carrasco's picture frames to a teenager's yet-to-fill-out shoulders leaves him wishing things could be different for his own family.

He does not want to think of his son, Alejandro, but he cannot avoid it, his son who was several years younger than the key-cutting teenager, but a heavy kid, always heavy. Even when his son was a baby, Santiago had wondered in private about what the boy would look like years down the line, and he had watched in growing dismay as Alejandro slowly rounded in the arms and legs, his cheeks bulging. In the summers, at the hotel pools, he'd watched each year as Alejandro splashed around with Eva, his red swim trunks with the elastic waist still unable to control the rolls of fat, his widening chest beginning to droop and sag. By the tenth summer, his boy was entering the pool wearing a long white T-shirt.

"Just leave him be," Luisa had told Santiago the day he came home from work after stopping at a sporting-goods store. She had peeked in the bag and tsk-tsked between her teeth. "He doesn't even like baseball."

At the school, Santiago parks the truck and takes down his toolbox and the new key chambers. He thinks ahead to the long work of transforming all the doors, the monotony of every change, the testing and turning of each key in the set, the pencil check on the paper to keep the record straight. Once in the building, he stares at the long hallway of empty classrooms, thinks of the supply closets on either end of the hall, the electrical rooms, rooms within rooms. Deep within some of the older buildings, he knows, are doors that haven't been opened in years, doors with lock chambers from years ago, detective-novel keyholes that will have to be replaced completely. Doors within doors within doors.

"Come here," Santiago had called that late afternoon after work, motioning to Alejandro and showing him the brand-new glove from the bag. "What do you think?"

Alejandro had looked at the glove but hadn't taken it until Santiago nudged it into his hands. He had tried putting it on his right hand. "It doesn't fit," Alejandro had said, and handed it back.

Santiago had smiled. "It goes on the other hand." He pulled his son's left arm toward him. "There. It should fit. Bend it a little."

It looked like a claw, a lobster grabbing and flexing as Alejandro clenched and released, the leather squeaking a bit as it moved.

"So what do you think?"

"I can't throw."

Santiago dug into the bag again. "I'll teach you," he said, and showed him his own brand-new glove. A matching pair. One adult, one child. "It's the same one," he said to Alejandro. "Try this one on."

Alejandro smiled as he tried it on, his row of white teeth, straight as soldiers, tiny and overwhelmed by the flesh of his cheeks. The bigger glove dwarfed his hand. He had been only nine years old. That was only four years ago.

In the bag were a softball and a baseball, and Santiago took the bigger one, leading Alejandro to the backyard. "We'll practice with this one first. It's softer and easier to catch. Now, stay right there." He pointed and then walked to the other edge of their yard. "Just hold out your glove."

Santiago knelt down, the grass cool against his knees. Alejandro stood the same way he had in the house, arm outstretched, the glove extended open and as useless as a broken claw. He pointed to the ball when it came to him, his feet stuck to the ground.

"That's all right," Santiago assured him. "Just move to the ball. Throw it back," he instructed. "Look at me. Aim at me." The ball wobbled back, but when Santiago caught it, there wasn't that sound. That sound of the ball smacking into the middle of the glove, the sound it made when he and his brother used to play with their father. They had played out in the backyard of their old house, a grassless patch, dust everywhere. The ball had sailed through the air, curving or flat, fly ball or grounder, zipping no matter what. That hard sound, the result of a good arm knowing how to throw, of a wrist that knew to snap just when, knees that bent at the right time. Their father had taken his own glove off to shake his hand in mock pain. They all shared sodas afterward, on the porch that sagged sadly to the west, the smell of dirt on their hands.

With his own son, there was no fleetness, no movement, just standing on the green grass, arm outstretched, a glove waiting. Santiago had an image of him standing in the lonely stretches of an outfield, bored beyond belief, his Little League uniform spotless. He had none of the athletic gawkiness of a pitcher, all skinny arms and legs but still coordinated, nor was he a commanding little tank of a catcher, tossing his mask off every chance he got, mimicking what he'd seen on the televised baseball games. Kids were teasing him, Luisa had said late at night when they were in bed. "You don't know what he goes through."

Santiago walked over to him. "Put your arm lower," he said, pushing Alejandro's elbow gently and forcing it to bend. "Just like that. Now, just grab at the ball when it comes. It won't hurt. I promise."

They threw that way for a while, Santiago aiming for the glove, then testing him a little, bouncing the ball or veering the toss a bit in either direction. Alejandro closed his eyes as the ball came toward him, the ball sometimes ricocheting from glove to ground. A few times, he was lucky enough to clutch at the ball just when it came into the pocket, and he opened his eyes in surprise, grinning at the glove as if it had done the work. Most of the time, both of them scrambled around on the grass, Alejandro missing the toss, Santiago stretching to block the ball from leaving the yard after one of Alejandro's errant throws.

Luisa watched from the back door, her gaze steady and determined. Santiago could feel her eyes from behind the shadowy frame of the window. But what did she know? How could she understand the cruelty of boys in private, the shenanigans in locker rooms, the mockery? He imagined girls did these things secretly, their jokes hidden behind shushed mouths, sly looks. Eva would be good at it. Boys were different in their ruthlessness, collectively rooting out a scapegoat, and who better to pick on than Alejandro, fast moving into his adolescence with all his baby fat still not gone. Santiago hated how Luisa called it baby fat, making it sound benign, something out of the boy's control. He threw the ball a little harder, hoping to hear a solid smack in Alejandro's glove — just one, just one hint that Alejandro was able to understand the importance of controlling one's own body, of commanding an instrument that transformed everything in life. A body didn't have to be sculpted in muscle, but it had to be active, mobile, capable, a way to carry oneself into the world, a posture.

"Come here," Santiago told him after the last toss. He met Alejandro midway across the lawn and led him to the back step, where Luisa quietly moved away from the doorframe, pretending she hadn't been watching. She busied herself at the kitchen sink, running the water and tinkling glasses against each other. But she soon stopped. She wanted to hear what they were talking about.

Alejandro breathed heavily, taking off the glove and handing it to Santiago.

"It's yours," Santiago said. "It doesn't fit me." He sat down on the back step, motioning for his son to sit with him. "So do you want to try again tomorrow?"

"I guess," Alejandro replied, shrugging his shoulders, so that momentarily they stuck up like two little jagged points despite his fleshiness.

"Did you like it?"

"Yeah," he answered, but not convincingly.

"You know, I used to play with your grandpa and your uncle when I was little."

"Uncle Luis?"

"Yeah. Every day. Your grandpa taught us how to throw and catch, and then he would take us out to the vacant lots and show us how to hit the ball. It was a lot of fun."

"Were you good at it?" Alejandro asked, and Santiago was surprised at the immediacy of the question.

"Yes, I guess. Your uncle was better, though. He won two trophies when he was little. Ask him to show them to you the next time we go over." Inside, he could hear Luisa pouring liquid into glasses. "Would you ever want a trophy like that? Wouldn't it be cool?"

Alejandro shrugged again, and when he did, Santiago felt a pang of guilt for asking him the question. Of course he would. Any kid would. But he knew from his son's shrug that such a trophy was already out of his reach, a desire best left to kids moving toward another horizon. It was unfair of him to baldly ask about such a wish, to ask about what secretly lurked in his son's mind.

"You want some lemonade?" Luisa asked, opening the back door. She held two glasses.

"Bring him some water, no?" Santiago asked, glancing down at his son's head, Alejandro's black hair shimmering dark against the fading daylight of the backyard. Luisa eyed Santiago, but went back inside. His boy could change. There were so many years ahead. He didn't say anything to Luisa when she came back out with two glasses of water, handing his to him coldly but stroking the back of Alejandro's hair with a gentle, proud assurance. Santiago sucked on an ice cube, turned his eyes to look at his boy's big head and his round calves tight against his jeans. Alejandro drank his water and set the glass down on the spongy grass, hunching over. His back seemed to arch up and out, like an alley cat's in Halloween pictures. Santiago put out his hand and gingerly straightened the boy's back. "You should sit up straight," he said, and kept his hand on Alejandro's back a bit longer than he needed to.

Lost in that moment, Santiago has forgotten his count. He is trying to remember how many doors he has finished — eight, nine? — when he hears the footsteps echoing at the end of the long corridor. At first, squinting to focus on the face, Santiago cannot tell who it is, but then he realizes the teenager is making his way toward him.

"Hey, Mr. Salinas," the teenager calls out halfway down the hall. "They sent me down here to start testing doors."

"I've been testing them," he replies, maybe a little too defensively. "They're all working."

"There's a whole bunch of other keys I have to check out. A grand master key, a master, a submaster."

"What the hell am I doing, then? What are these?" Santiago points to his own stash of keys.

"Those keys are for the teachers," the teenager explains. "It's a system. The grand master opens everything in the district, but the master opens every door in only this building . . ."

"Save it." Santiago waves at him and kneels back down to the key chamber he was replacing. "Do what you need to do. Just leave me alone," he mutters, and the teenager walks off down the hall. Santiago can hear keys jingling, the slide of the brass into each lock, the knobs twisted vigorously, then the kid moving on to the next door in satisfaction. Santiago slides the latest chamber into place and tries to work faster, but he knows the kid will catch up to him eventually. For a moment, he visualizes himself back at the warehouse, the teenager sitting down next to him, explaining how the key system for the entire district is going to work, the kid's fingers running dexterously past a list of numbers, Santiago himself staring blankly at the pages.

"Mr. Salinas?" the teenager calls out. "This door down here. Did your key work?"

"Of course it did," he replies. "I moved on, didn't I?"

"My key doesn't work. It's supposed to open everything."

"Well, maybe you made a mistake." Santiago peeks into the classroom he has just finished. Because it has no interior closets, he picks up his toolbox and starts down the hall to the next door.

"It's not possible," the teenager calls out. "The keys I'm using should open everything on this floor."

"I'm telling you I did what I was supposed to do."

One more time, the teenager jiggles at the locked door, trying his set of keys. Santiago works faster, putting extra muscle into his screwdriver, breaking past some paint carelessly sealed over the metalwork. He dislodges his latest doorknob, starts extracting the key chamber, keeping his eye on the kid down the hall.

Finally, whether he built up enough courage or simply knew he had to ask Santiago for help, the teenager starts to walk down the hall, the rubber of his sneakers squeaking against the floors. "Mr. Salinas," he says, stopping short. "Can I check the keys you used? In the box?"

"Which one?"

"They're all labeled," the kid answers quickly. And curtly — his voice carries the hurried, swallowed quality of facing down a bully, a voice perfectly suited to these halls, and it's this voice that corners Santiago.

Santiago knows he has made a mistake and the kid knows how the keys work better than he does. He fumbles around the box with the tiny manila envelopes. "This one," he says, handing it to him.

"It's the wrong one. This should have gone on the second floor, not this one." The kid points to the label. "See?"

"Fucking change it yourself, then."

The kid looks at him as if he might have been joking, but quickly realizes Santiago is serious, and he gathers his things. Santiago knows he's in for it when the teenager almost shrugs as he turns away and begins the walk down the hall, his perfect keys jingling, the door closing ominously behind him. Carrasco will be on his way soon.

In the corner of the next classroom there is a little closet, and after replacing the lock on the hallway door and testing it, Santiago walks toward the closet. Tempted to close the door behind him, all the harder for Carrasco to find him, he thinks the better of it. He will no doubt hear Carrasco's angry footsteps all the way down the hall, but so far there is only quiet, and Santiago calms himself, choosing not to rehearse a defense. Carrasco should understand. Who wants to take orders from a fucking kid?

The door before him, though, takes his mind off the impending confrontation. Curiously, the keyhole has been painted over and the doorknob doesn't turn in either direction. The paint on the door has been slathered on so thickly and so many times over the years that he'll have to destroy a hefty chunk of the door just to get it open. Santiago gets to work, chipping away at some of the paint, dislodging one of the screws. He studies the knob closely, the shape of it. Such an old fixture, he thinks, that it may be worth something, may be worth sneaking it home if he can keep it intact. Loosened, the doorknob slips out, and the door is left with a gaping hole in the lock; still, it is sealed shut. Frustrated, Santiago grabs a hammer and starts cracking at the wood around the fixture, the sound echoing into the hallway. He doesn't hear Carrasco come into the classroom, and he almost drops the tools in surprise when Carrasco speaks.

"Tough one, huh?" Carrasco says from behind him.

"Oh, it's a son of a bitch, all right."

"Need help?"

"Got it," Santiago says, pounding harder, thankful that the wood finally gives way. He cracks open the door, the paint seal all around the doorframe flaking away. "Wonder what's in here." He steps inside.

"Books," Carrasco says, leaning his head in. A small closet, the room has a window on one side, left open all these years just enough to allow a layer of dirt to cake itself to the sill. Lined with wooden shelves, the closet holds books numbered and neatly stacked. Small cobwebs sway as the first faint gusts of air come from the classroom. Santiago looks up to the ceiling; sure enough, the light fixture holds one of the old translucent bulbs, the clear glass showing the filament radiant inside.

"Fucking teachers," Carrasco says, still leaning inside. "Always complaining about not having books. Look at this treasure."

Santiago pokes around the books, wiping away at the heavy dust to read the covers. *Edith Hamilton's Mythology. A Separate Peace.* Carrasco is quiet, but Santiago knows he is still there.

"You gotta lay off the kid," Carrasco tells him finally. "You gotta take it easy."

"He just got the envelopes mixed up, you know. He's a kid," he tries, but Carrasco isn't buying it.

"A really smart one. Superintendent's nephew. Who do you think got him that cushy little job, instead of him out cutting grass like the rest of them?"

Santiago turns around, his investigation of the shelves exhausted. Carrasco stands in the doorway, arms crossed in front of him.

"Salinas, you need a break, man. You're mouthing off to a fucking kid."

Santiago sighs and moves to the doorway, but Carrasco doesn't budge.

"Take a week off. You've got days."

"I don't need a break," he tells Carrasco. He puts his hand on the broken door, readying himself to change the subject, talk about how they'll need to get somebody in here to clean up the mess inside, make the closet usable again.

"After all that's happened, man?" Carrasco asks. "You're telling me you don't need a little time? It's been months. Why don't you just get a little time away?"

"Luisa and I separated," he tells him, the words coming forth as both an admission and a prayer that Carrasco will now leave him alone. Instead, unexpectedly, Santiago feels a quiver in his left knee, feels the heat of the closet on his neck and face, the lump in his throat, gathering there at the admission.

"I heard," Carrasco says quietly, shifting a little but making no movement toward him. "It's a tough thing to go through, losing a son like that." He pauses as if to gauge whether what he has said is enough, but Santiago keeps his head down, concentrating on the dusty floor and a spider scurrying from one of the shelves.

"Come on out here." Carrasco motions, opening the closet door, which creaks and groans, releasing more of the old paint. "Sit," he tells Santiago, taking one of the desks himself.

Neither of them can fit comfortably in the students' desks anymore; they sit sideways.

"You never took bereavement," Carrasco tells him. "Just put in for it. Take a week. I can talk to the main office and explain. They have the records."

"What am I going to do for a week?"

"Relax. Think a little." Carrasco inspects the corroded paint around the doorframe. "Talk to your lady. Settle some things."

"It's too late."

"Never too late. Not when you're married." Carrasco sighs. It is his wife who buys the shirts with the tiny check pattern, the lilac tinge. It is she who holds him together, Santiago can tell. "Besides," Carrasco says, "everybody wonders what's going on with you. You just came back after it happened. Not a day off."

Santiago looks around the classroom, sensing somehow that this is a freshman English class. Wasn't that the year he had toted around *A Separate Peace*, a book he couldn't get more than a few pages into, his eyes wandering over the spine to Luisa, more dutiful in her reading? Carrasco seems patient enough, waiting for an answer, and Santiago takes in the room, the pristine summer blackboards, the last prizewinning essays still stapled to one of the walls, a flag fluttering.

"Come on," Carrasco says, rising. "Don't even worry about signing out. I'm sending you home. The guys can take care of these floors."

Alejandro would have entered high school in September, Santiago thinks. He would have sat in a classroom much like this. But it is July, and there will be time enough to think about that when September comes, when he sees the teenagers making their way along the sidewalks, pushing each other and horsing around. He closes his toolbox and starts to follow Carrasco down the hallway, but then remembers the ornate doorknob. Doubling back, Santiago stuffs it into his toolbox and follows once again, leaving the classroom door wide open behind him.

There will be time enough in September, he tells himself. There will be time enough today even, the morning only halfway through. "I'll go in your truck," Carrasco says, leaving his own vehicle there. "I'll come back with one of the guys." The drive to the warehouse is silent. After parking the truck, Santiago unloads his toolbox and heads to the warehouse doors. He can see the teenager sneaking a glance at him through the office window, but he won't give him the satisfaction of acknowledgment. Nor will he look up at the guys milling around the soda machine, taking their time so they can eavesdrop. They think he is being let go. A week from now, Santiago knows, some of them will have to eat crow when they find out he was sent on bereavement leave and not fired.

The drive home is quick, no traffic now that everyone has made it to work. Home is empty, cavernous almost with its yawning rooms, Luisa gone, Eva with her, the door to Alejandro's room unopened for months. His steps sound strangely loud, even against carpet. Santiago takes a quick shower, though he hasn't broken much of a sweat. For the journey, he wants to feel clean, to enter the hotel in fresh clothes, assured of belonging. He chooses a long-sleeved white shirt and khaki trousers and presses them the way his mother showed him. In the back corner of the closet, past his regular, dark dress shoes, are a pair of brown leather sandals — Luisa's idea — and he takes those out to wear even though they make him feel slightly effeminate. Not knowing how long he will be gone, and refusing to make himself consider it, he hauls down a suitcase from the top of the closet and folds in enough clothing for a week, along with his favorite pair of black dress shoes.

Ready, Santiago trails the suitcase behind him and gathers his keys and wallet from the kitchen table. Luisa has not called him in several weeks, and Eva pays him little mind. Nevertheless he digs out pen and paper from one of the kitchen drawers. *Luisa, I'm going out of town for a few days to think things over. Maybe we can talk when I get back.* For a moment, he considers what he has written, tries to imagine Luisa coming to the house to find him and seeing the note, tucked here on the counter under a glass. But the house is pristine in its emptiness—the things she has taken, the little he has done in his day-to-day life since she left with Eva. The kitchen counter is spotless. He rinses his breakfast dishes every morning, the sink empty, a small drop collecting at the faucet and then giving way, its watery echo in the grand silence of the house. Santiago crumples up the note and tries again. *Luisa, I needed to get out.* He sets the note down, puts the glass over it. It matters little what the words say. The note will remain there, untouched.

Nostalgia, the will of memory to rectify everything—what a weakness, he thinks. But Santiago gets in the car nonetheless, feeling an eagerness to get going on the drive. It's just past noon and the traffic will be light all the way to the coast. There is no use pretending that the drive will quiet what's in his head. Already he is starting with comparisons and he has yet to even gas up for the trip. How empty the car feels this time, when in the past the kids argued in the backseat and Luisa fiddled with the radio stations.

At the mini-mart in the center of town, he buys snacks for the road and fills up the tank. The gas is more expensive here: it's mostly high school kids who come to buy chips and sodas, but summer has a lulling effect, and Santiago wants the calm start, the slow ease into what is coming. He travels down the main street following the speed limit, and the car behind him angrily pulls up to his rear bumper, trying to nudge him along. People are going about their day: shopping on foot if they live on the south side, hanging around the corner hoping for under-the-table construction jobs. Mexican kids are practicing on skateboards, of all things. He drives by the barbershop, the lone Chinese restaurant with its pale aqua storefront, the ninety-nine-cent store, the church-sponsored thrift shop. The stores crumble down as he gets closer to the main road leading to the highway: just the tire shop now, the car wash, a tractor rental place. His town gives way to farmland, an open road that will take him back to the hotel for no other reason than to let him face his mistake, his error, and to ask the sea, the Pacific sky, for a little peace in the matter.

The farmland slips along and he hits the other side of Highway 41, the old part that snakes into the western foothills, the dry flatlands cut through with the vague outline, way out there in the distance, of a canal carrying mountain runoff to the farmers of the West Valley and on down to Los Angeles. Santiago sets the radio to an oldies station, the only music everyone in the car could agree on, and he catches Connie Francis in the middle of her spiteful mourning. The music keeps the thinking out of his head, and mercifully, the station's DJ rarely interrupts except to announce a stretch of music. He keeps waiting for the station to throw in something too upbeat and whistle-clean like the Association or the Beach Boys, but he begins to suspect that the DJ is a romantic of the old kind, his age, who knew the music he and Luisa listened to when they were dating, parking up at Avocado Lake and looking down at the Valley lights while listening to the radio. The brown flatlands start to give way to gentle hills, yellowing grass, but still the music comes. The Delfonics and Eddie Holman's rueful yearning, and Eva's favorite, Billy Paul singing about Mrs. Jones. It will be at least an hour until Kettleman City, the lone town on this stretch of highway cutting over to the coast, and Santiago puts his hand on the empty passenger seat when the Stylistics sing "You Make Me Feel Brand New," as if this were the very car he had kissed Luisa in all those years ago.

But by Kettleman City, the radio station fades to a static, the tune coming in spurts, and Santiago finally has to turn it off and sit through the silence. Here, then, is the long climb, the treacherous road. He can see it miles ahead—the road climbing in a straight shot to the top of the first hill, where he knows for miles on end the highway will twist, climb, and dip and the car will speed on its own, commanded by gravity. It will take concentration to handle this part of the journey, his eyes focused on the painted yellow lines on the asphalt, but Santiago is already at his destination, at the base of the swimming pool all those months ago, he and Luisa sitting in lounge chairs under the afternoon sun. Three elderly Russian women, rotund in their sundresses and yet somehow still looking frail, sat under the shade of a palm tree, one of them telling a story to the other two. Their heads nodded collectively, as if they shared in the memory, had no doubt that each recalled it with the same precision. The two women hummed as the third told her story. Yes, their heads nodded, yes. The third woman remembered best of all, yes. And then she began to sing, at which Luisa turned as if annoyed, but Santiago listened to the song, not understanding, but knowing what the melody invoked.

He had lost himself in lounging that day, in listening, when Eva and Alejandro came to the edge of the pool, hot and sweat-streaked from whatever they had been doing. Even before Alejandro had put his first foot in, Santiago called him over. "Not with the shirt on," he told him. "You need something dry to wear to dinner."

"But I have a shirt upstairs," Alejandro had protested, his voice loud, breaking through the gentle atmosphere the three Russian women had created around the pool.

"Do as I say and stop being such a baby."

"Leave him alone," Luisa told Santiago. "He's got one upstairs, he told you."

What drove Santiago to get up from his chaise lounge was the way Alejandro turned around, as if Luisa's word were the decree: the son would have his way. What drove him to get up and reach for his brown leather sandal was watching the wide, sagging back of his son turning and making his way to the pool, self-satisfied. Without warning, as if Alejandro hadn't heard him walking up from behind, Santiago smacked him with the sandal on the exposed part of his lower leg, his shorts long and baggy.

Alejandro cried out in surprise, his hand around the spot where he'd been hit. The elderly Russian women turned in their chairs to watch. "You do as I say," Santiago told him. "Do not make me hit you again."

"I have another shirt . . . ," he began, the words long and drawn out and whining, but Santiago did not let him finish. He smacked him again, harder, egged on by his own frustration, and this time Alejandro began to cry, then bolted from the pool.

"Now see what you did?" Luisa admonished. "Just lay off of him, Santiago, for God's sake."

"You baby him," Santiago told her, sitting back down. "I'm getting really sick of his shit," he said, regretting his words almost immediately. He could see Eva out of the corner of his eye, leaving the pool area. She'd overheard him.

"You don't know what his life is like outside of us, outside of the house. You don't think the kids are teasing him at school? Day in, day out." Luisa took off her sunglasses and shook them at him. "Eva tells me all the time about those damn kids picking on him. You don't have to contribute to it."

"He's got to grow up," Santiago insisted. "You have to grow a spine sometime." They both sat in the lounges, but his skin flushed with anger and the sun seemed to beat down on him unbearably. He wanted to stand his ground with Luisa, though, and refused to head to the pool.

"Mom!" Eva called. Her voice was tiny. "Mom!" It was coming from the balcony and they all looked up: Santiago, Luisa, the elderly Russian women shading their eyes, squinting to look up at Eva on the eighth-floor balcony, frantically waving her hands to get their attention. "Mom!" she yelled.

"Goddamn," Luisa muttered. "You see what you started up?"

She gathered her towel and slipped on her sandals. She exited the pool area, and Santiago tried not to look at the Russian women, who eyed him with a withering contempt. One of them kept her eyes shaded, looking upward, as if Eva were still on the balcony, but his daughter made no further noise to warrant such attention. It is only now, as Santiago hurtles toward Paso Robles, toward the turn onto the coastal highway that will take him back to the hotel, that he imagines the old woman looking up as if with prescience. The singing woman, the one who had continued to look up, had been the one to shout first, a terrible, guttural cry summoned from the terror of the things she must have witnessed in her day. The other two women instantaneously turned and shrieked, and Santiago himself cocked his head, looking upward now, only to see his son plummeting down from the balcony, his legs and arms flailing as if in disbelief at what he had just done, in disbelief that he could not, in fact, reverse himself. Luisa and Eva appeared on the balcony, sudden as apparitions, crying out, their bodies leaning forward as if they could somehow catch Alejandro. All of them were caught paralyzed at the sickening distance, the pitch of the boy's body, the inevitable thudding on the pavement, the terrible wait. The Russian women cried out as if in pain, and Santiago began running, his heart jarring — breaking — at the sound of Alejandro slamming into the edge of the pool's deck. He ran, guided by the echo of Luisa's wailing from the balcony, Eva's voice suddenly that of a little girl. He ran to kneel beside his son's body, the entire collapse and crush of Alejandro's bones, the blood trickle warm against his knees. He does not remember a sound coming out of his own mouth, not until the paramedics came, their hands futilely checking for a pulse.

Up ahead is the hotel, the tower of it gleaming in the late afternoon sunshine. A barge lingers offshore, so far away that Santiago cannot tell if it is moving north or south. He, though, is moving with clarity, with purpose, the hotel beckoning in the way only memory can. He remembers it all: the sweep of the lobby large for such a tiny hotel. The front desk in a sunken area of red carpet, its phone almost apologetic in its quiet ring. It will be just as he remembers. The room number, 806, in a diamond-shaped placard, and the lemon-colored walls, the door painted a forest green, so deep and green against the brass. The large beds with their antique-style headboards, the coverlets a soft beige, not the garish floral patterns that hotels usually present. The sea air, the look down onto the pool. Back then, in February, five o'clock would have meant the sun was going down, but it is now July. The sun is still in force. The coast, though, will be just as it was then, the temperature never deviating much from its mild norm. The palm trees sway a bit in the parking lot, where the slots are mostly empty.

At the front desk, the young woman asks him for a reservation number, but he does not have one. "We'll have something for you," she says, nonplussed. "I've got a nonsmoking on the third floor."

"If you have room 806, I'll take that," he tells her, and when she looks back at him inquisitively, he says, "My wife and I . . . we stayed in that room before."

She taps at the keyboard. "Yes, that's a big room. It's available," she says, and makes her adjustment. She slides over the check-in forms and clicks a pen for him, giving him a small envelope.

"What's this?"

"Card key," she says. "Do you need another for your wife?"

He signs the forms. "We had keys before. Real keys." He twists his hand at her, as if she needed a demonstration.

"We renovated this spring," the young woman tells him, grinning. "People were always losing the regular keys and it was getting too expensive to replace locks. Card keys are better for security anyway—makes our guests feel safer."

"I suppose so," Santiago says, and heads to the elevator bank without prompting. He is disappointed that it will not be the same, not exactly the same. He wants the elderly Russian women to be down at the poolside, quietly singing through their previous devastations. He knows what he is seeking in this return, a kind of redeeming exile, but as the elevator climbs to the eighth floor, Santiago knows his quest is as futile as changing direction midair. Decisions have been made and they are irreversible. Luisa will never come back. He can picture her, though, even now as he makes his way down the breezeway to room 806. His wife kneeling at one of the beds in their hotel room, Eva crying and struggling to contain her mother's shaking. "Please forgive him, Lord," he could hear Luisa saying. "Please forgive him, Lord." He had not known whom she was referring to at first, her tears stifled by the repetition, her insistence. Eva had turned to look at him, her hands tightening on her mother's shoulders as if to warn her. But Luisa had paid neither of them any mind. "Please forgive him, Lord. Remember him, Lord, when you come into your kingdom."

At the door, he slides the card key in and the electronic lock lights momentarily, inviting him to click open. He does, and there is the room. There are the beds with the soft beige sheets. There are the paintings on the wall: he wills himself to remember the scenes, a young milkmaid accepting a boy's offer of love, her face twisted away in shame. Back there is the bathroom, the dark space, the door now open, but that is where Alejandro had been. That is where, Luisa told him later, he had gone to cry, the locked door alarming her. That is the door that had swung open when she raised her voice, Alejandro bolting out — "as if the devil had gotten into him, that look in his eye, I'll never forget," said Luisa — and running for the balcony. This very balcony. Santiago stands in the archway of the room for a long time, the door ajar, surveying, afraid to go near the edge of the breezeway. He does not trust his memory. The outside walls are indeed lemon yellow. But the door is white.

Santiago knows he has come here to understand how Alejandro could have looked at such a miraculous horizon — the sheer blue line of the ocean meeting its own impossible expanse — and seen, instead, an exit. He does not trust Luisa's account of what happened and wishes, somehow, that he could have seen it all for himself. He would've done more than just stand there. Look at the distance from the bathroom to the open doorway, the steps along the breezeway, the height of the balcony wall. He could have stopped him. He pictures his son in the sudden burst of a runner from a starting block, his body racing from the end of the room, relentless, the lift in his legs coming from a diamond-muscled calf, his legs extending, his arms graceful in giving himself a heave, a vault into his own understanding.

But it wasn't so. It was sloppy, clumsy, a gesture tripped up by fear. Santiago knows it was, because he stands there contemplating what it would take to make the same leap. A fearful space opens in his stomach at the thought, his body bracing against the doorway. Santiago has to hang on to the doorframe, as if his body could make a decision his mind could not refuse. And yet his feet will not yield, will not allow him to close the door and sit in the room, resist the danger. He stands in place long enough for the late afternoon to slowly give way to the early evening. There, now, is the fog gathering faintly. There is the barge, so far away, its destination still imperceptible. There is the sun beginning its embrace of the horizon, its dark time coming, its rest. The ocean shimmers with the pink light, the brassy orange, the sun made strangely brighter as it fights the fog.

Santiago sees how his son saw. He is in the growing dark of the hotel room with the door open and it is midweek in July. No one has passed on the breezeway. The hotel is empty. The elderly Russian women are gone, each with a new vision to trouble her sleep, so late in life. There are no sounds coming from the pool, only the lonely rasping of the palm fronds. Santiago stands there and sees how he is not capable of forgiving himself, but at least he accepts his own fear. His son was a lonely child. Santiago accepts that he is lonely, too, and always has been. Loneliness is greater than any anger, any shame he has ever felt. Greater, in fact, than love. He can see how his son saw, and he knows what it is to be him and prove incapable of resisting his own body, how his hands and feet could move forward as if on their own.

The sun gives way. The orange glares for a moment, then disappears, leaving the sky to soften into reds and pinks. A thin fog rolls toward shore, but everything loses out to the violet of nightfall, the ocean contributing its own darkness. He does not know what to do with the terrible pain he has carried within himself for these months. *It is nothing but guilt, and that goes away in time,* Santiago's hands whisper to him. He has to get a grip on himself. Shame goes away. Anger goes away. Fear goes away. Lust goes away, too. Yes, even love. He sees the elderly Russian women nodding silently in agreement, yes. Even love.

TELL HIM ABOUT BROTHER JOHN

EVERY TRIP BACK FROM Over There is a wreck of anxiety. Every trip back, I used to be welcomed home eagerly and with open arms, but today it is only my father, subdued, babysitting the nephews. Over There is "Allá," the way my father says it and then tips his chin at the horizon. Right there. As if the place he means to talk about is either across the street or too far away to imagine. My mother is Over There: she packed her belongings and left with another man, headed for a big city. It's a different Allá, a different Over There, but the way my father tips his chin is the same. It isn't here. I love my mother still, but I wish she would come home sometimes, just so she knows how this feels, this coming back, this answering for the way things are.

My father takes care of the nephews, and they start immediately with too many questions about living Over There, the romanticizing of its danger, its enormity. My nephews watch old Charles Bronson movies on television, still popular on the local stations in the midafternoon. They ask me if my life is like this: stolen drugs and brutalized girlfriends and guns illuminating the night streets. My oldest nephew is only ten years old.

I started saying Allá, too, because I was embarrassed about it. "Here," I say, giving one of the lighter suitcases to my oldest nephew. "Put that in the bedroom for me." It pains me to hear my nephews ask such stupid questions, the way their young hearts believe that I'm lying to them and holding back the details of a life filled with excitement and anticipations. My life is this: I'm broke, cramped in my apartment, on edge in the late night – early morning hours, convinced I'm missing out on some unimaginable vitality somewhere in the city. I say nothing to my nephews or my father about my job, but then again they hardly ever ask.

Every year, when the tiny plane descends, bringing me back into the flat arid interior of the Valley, back to the house I grew up in on this street, when my nephews climb on my every limb to welcome me home, I think I might be yearning. But then a fear comes over me, a feeling of being fooled and hypnotized by nostalgia. Sometimes I imagine Gold Street as a living being, an entity with arms waiting. Sometimes I imagine waking up Over There, parting my curtains, and seeing not the shadowy city streets but the plum blossoms and the Chinese elms, the paper-boys tossing the morning news, cycling down Gold Street at the point in the neighborhood where you can do a U-turn and not a three-point. All of that imagining gives me a tight, constricted feeling.

"So who's called?" I ask my father, and try to shoo the boys away.

"Your cousin Oscar, your tía Carolina. Your grandpa Eugenio. Your sister wants to show you the new baby." My father shakes his head. "Can you believe it? Seven boys and still no girl."

My nephews run back down the hallway toward me, all of their tiny hands grabbing at a basketball, ready for a game on the dirt driveway. My father has built them a hoop out of a large plastic bucket and a piece of plywood. "Not now," I say, sending them out. "Maybe later." I send them out even though there isn't much to say to my father. My father, as if he knows this, too, goes over to the phone and starts making a spate of calls, announcing my safe arrival.

I wait patiently on the couch, looking around at the house, which is becoming more unfamiliar, bit by bit, with every trip home. At the back of the kitchen, where the door opens out onto the garage and the dirt driveway, one of my nephews bounds back inside. I can hear his voice, already breathless and heated. I can hear the refrigerator door open, the sound of thirst being quenched. He's drinking cherry punch — some things do not change. I can hear my nephew's voice, but I'm embarrassed to admit that I cannot tell which one it is. My father is still on the telephone, but my nephew asks him anyway, "Did you tell him about Brother John?"

BROTHER JOHN ISN'T MY brother. He isn't anyone's brother, though all of us on Gold Street claim him as one of ours. This is why, whenever I come home, I'm obligated to see him.

Brother John, then and now, is the same person he has always been. He was the boy in town with no parents, no family. He had been held under the care of various aunts and uncles in some of the other small towns, always being shuttled back and forth between Orange Cove and Sanger and Parlier and even Pixley, his clothes carried in a single paper sack. Everyone on Gold Street watched from behind window curtains whenever he was brought back to the neighborhood to stay with the Márquez family, everyone shaking their heads about how poorly dressed he was, how underfed. Long after the Márquez family moved away — back to Mexico, some said — the car with Brother John came back and stopped at the empty house. The two women who had driven Brother John there knocked on the door; then one of them went back to the car and beeped the horn. They kept honking until one of the neighbors came over, told them that no one was living there, and then claimed Brother John, just like that. Our next-door neighbors, in fact. The car that brought Brother John drove away, and from then on, we were all instructed to treat Brother John as if he were one of our own.

I was too young then to know about legalities and I'm too old now to ask something so improper, something that is none of my business. Rumors about Brother John flew all around, but they were not mean spirited. They were things we asked only among ourselves, and it was understood that we were never to mention our questioning to him. Was he from Mexico? Did his parents abandon him? Were his parents dead? Why didn't his aunts or uncles want him? Was he sick? Did our neighbors get money from the government to keep him? Had we all noticed how the neighbors drove new cars every couple of years, ever since they had taken in Brother John? Why didn't he look like anybody in town, where cousins lived around almost every corner? Did his parents love him?

"You should go next door," my father says to me, "and see if Brother John is home."

I try to think of some excuse to delay the obligatory visit, but there is no avoiding it, not with my father. Even though my mother left him, my father is still a well-respected man in town. He is a war veteran; he marches in all the town parades, holding the American flag. He attends Saturday breakfasts at the Iglesia de San Pedro, where the town elders raise funds. He sits on the town council and reviews applications for new businesses: always yes to franchise restaurants, always no to the new liquor stores. I can wait only so long before I have to go next door to see Brother John. It's expected, because of who my father is, that I not be arrogant.

I can hear my nephews arguing in the driveway. They are still young. I wonder when my father will start coming down on them.

I KNOCK ON THE heavy black security door and I hear shuffling in the living room. "Who is it?" says Doña Paulina in her broken English, and when I call out to her that it's me, she parts the curtain as if to make sure. She opens the door and motions me in, but she isn't smiling—I've never liked her. I point to my car next door, as if it were running and ready to go. "Brother John?"

"¡Juanito!" she calls out, holding the door open, wiping one hand clean on her apron. The living room looks much smaller than I remember it.

"Hey," Brother John says, emerging from the hallway. His room is in the back, the same room. We're twenty-six now, both of us, and it flashes through me: why is he still here, when he had a chance to get away? He got away, actually—to Oklahoma—but he came back. "Your dad told me you were coming to visit."

"Yeah," I tell him. "Hey, do you want to get a bite to eat? Just here in town?"

Doña Paulina stands staring at both of us. I know she understands what we're saying, and even though I've never liked the woman, I respect her. Brother John is no one's flesh and blood, not on this street, but she raised him when she didn't have to.

"Sure," Brother John says, walking to the door without gathering anything, as if he had been expecting the invitation. He extends his hand and I shake it; it's thick and hot. Neither of us lets go, and I'm almost afraid to: it's as if my father were in the room and not next door. I can imagine the town elders talking to my father on Saturday morning: "¿Y tu hijo? When is he coming home?"

THE TRIP HOME FROM Over There will be only a week long. I will visit my ailing grandfather Eugenio between his afternoon naps and then drive back to my father's house feeling guilty about my grandpa's health. I will supervise my nephews as my father escapes with relief from this daily task my brothers and sisters put on him, knowing he feels too guilty to say no to their demands. My brothers and sisters will go to work, grateful for the savings in day care, but won't say thank you. It will mean an uncomfortable session with my father, a sitting-in-silence that means nothing except that my father is still thinking about my mother and how she abandoned him. Luckily, my high school friends Willy and Al will invite me over to Willy's place for beer and then me driving the car home drunk. It will mean, one morning at the grocery store, running into the girl who had a crush on me in high school — Lily still not married, still idling in the cul-de-sacs of the men she now wants, parking outside their houses and waiting through nothing. It will mean opening my town's thin paper and whistling at how much property you can get for only five figures and what a pushover I am for living Over There. During the week, I will have to nurse a pulled and aching hamstring from playing basketball with my nephews. They know the small dips and holes in the dirt driveway better than I do. It will mean resting on the sofa with my hamstring wrapped, leg raised, the house quiet, and next door Brother John, and the story he told me unable to be taken back.

• • •

BROTHER JOHN KNOWS WHERE the new places are and he directs me to one of the franchise restaurants in town, along the new strip mall that has sprouted on the east side, the painted stucco bright against the fresh parking lot, the cars eager with patrons. Everyone in town comes here now, avoiding the dilapidated downtown and its struggling stores. The strip mall is wide, neon lit, smooth tarred, convenient, sparely landscaped with fledgling trees and shrubs. I would never find a place like this Over There, and part of me is grateful for the proximity of all this, the wide space, the cleanliness and the order and the newness of everything in sight, everything an enormous city could never offer.

At the restaurant, we sit in a booth with comfortable cloth-covered seats, etched glass, and spacious tables. The young waiters circle quickly with hot dishes. I think of all my friends Over There and how they would deny that they come from such places. They feel a particular shame, I think, about coming from towns like this. But I'm glad for it: I think of my father and the town elders planning and hoping, counting the jobs at this restaurant, at the video store across the way, at the giant supermarket and the pharmacy. I wish I could be a little more like them or Doña Paulina, looking out for other people.

Brother John studies the menu, and while his eyes are downcast, I study him: he seems smaller, his shoulders narrowed, his chest caved. Because I've been Over There and know more than just Mexican faces, I see the mystery of his parents through his face. He has the wide face that we all have, and the dark skin, but his hair is fine — fine and brown. I don't remember it being brown. Beautiful, actually, the length of it creeping past his neck. With his face down, his eyes not showing, he could be a white boy, but I have never even tried to imagine who his parents could have been. None of the stories have ever convinced me.

"You look tired," I say to him.

Brother John sighs and closes the menu. "Tough lately." He looks up at me. "Being here." His eyes lock on mine. It's only Over There that people look me in the eye—that I feel okay about looking someone in the eye.

I look back down at my menu and don't say anything to Brother John. Our waiter takes a long time to come to our table, and I put on an act of not knowing what to order. For a while, it works; Brother John has little to say. But as soon as the waiter has come and taken our order, Brother John starts up, naming names, the people we went to school with. As with my friends Over There, I try to keep as much to myself as possible, only nod my head, try to avoid contributing to conjecture. It doesn't faze Brother John. He tells me that Agustina had a baby a year after high school and could never determine the father. "And word is, Ginger—that teacher's daughter—she had a baby, too, but no one knew about it and she gave it up for adoption. Beto and Patsy got married and then divorced, because Beto was having an affair with Carla—remember her? Carla Ysleta? Now Beto and Carla are married and Patsy's alone with no kids."

Brother John says all this without keeping his voice down, and I can sense people are cocking their ears for gossip. People know people in this town. People know.

"Violeta, of all the ones, never got married or had kids, but word was she couldn't have any and had depression for years. That happened to her sister, Sofía. Remember her? That's why a lot of people think she killed herself. And Emilio Rentería—he hurt himself so bad on night shift at the paper mill that he can't work anymore. But you can see him at the Little League games. He coaches the kids, even though he uses a wheelchair."

A friend of my father's passes by our table on his way out and extends his hand. "Good to see you," Señor Treviño says. He beams proudly at me, and behind his smile I can almost hear my father telling his lies to the old men at the Iglesia de San Pedro. "Say hello to your father." Brother John says nothing to him, does not meet his eyes, and it surprises me that Señor Treviño simply goes on his way, giving Brother John only a slight nod.

"What's that about?" I ask Brother John when the old man leaves the restaurant. "He knows you."

Brother John sniffs. "He thinks he does."

"What do you mean?"

"They're making me pay back the scholarship. Remember that?"

I do remember it. I remember the envy, the luck I thought he had, how the Iglesia de San Pedro had silently pushed their bake sales and Saturday breakfasts and tithing to present Brother John a check to attend a school in Oklahoma. My father had reprimanded me one night when I said something about how unfair it was: "You think about what that kid has been through. All his life. Who does he have to turn to except these people right here at the church?" My mother had been sitting on the couch watching her telenovela. She had rolled her eyes in disgust. That was the year before she left.

"Why are they making you pay it back?"

"I didn't finish," says Brother John, and he looks back down. His brown hair falls a little, but I can still see his face, and for the first time — maybe because I'm old enough now — I recognize what a sad life he has had, all the things he does not know. At least my mother, even though she is not with my father anymore, calls me. "Why are you Over There anyway?" she pleads, and right now, as I think of her and see Brother John's downcast eyes, her pleading is not a nuisance.

The waiter comes with the food, the plates hot, and I shovel the food in. I can sense it coming from Brother John, the need to say something, and I feel sorry for having asked him out to eat. He does not touch his food.

Finally, when I'm halfway through my plate, he picks up his fork and starts eating. "Did you think I was praying?" he asks.

I laugh nervously. I remember the school he was sent to, a religious school smack in the middle of Oklahoma.

His voice hushes a little and I have to lean in to hear him. He starts telling me, even while he's eating, but I can understand him. He doesn't swallow the words. "I got there, to Oklahoma, and I had that money. But I ran out real quick after I bought books and stuff, and I couldn't afford the dorms. So I found this room from a family that lived in the middle of town. When I told them I was a student down at the school, they let me stay real cheap. The room was upstairs, like an attic, and I had my own stairwell that ran above the garage. I had to be real careful in the rain. Or the snow. They had used this real cheap glossy paint on the wood and it was slippery. But they never bothered me. I still needed money, though, so I started tending bar without telling them, just to make some extra. Things were going fine for a long time, and then . . ."

I resist saying, *What?* My food is nearly gone, but Brother John takes his time. He pushes the fork around on his plate, takes a few small bites.

"I met someone," he says very quietly. "One of my classmates. He was from South Carolina."

He is telling me this because I'm living Over There; he thinks anywhere but here will let you live a life never allowed. He thinks Over There is full of people falling in love, people waiting to listen to you while you do the falling. He sees right through me, my moving Over There. But I still say nothing.

"His name was Gary. Gary Lee Brown. I met him and started seeing him a lot. And a few months later I lied to that family and told them that Gary needed help and could he stay with me, and they said yes. The father even helped us move Gary's bed up to that room, even though we never used it. We just set it up in case the family came upstairs, but they never did. The hard thing was, Gary was real religious. He believed it, I mean, and even after we'd been together like that for a year, he kept telling me that what we were doing was wrong, that it was a sin. He'd scare me sometimes, the things he'd say, like driving out in the middle of the wheat fields and just sitting, thinking about killing himself. 'You're just out there, thinking?' I would ask him when he'd come home late, real late—two in the morning, sometimes. And that's what would scare me, all those hours, being alone at night when I knew what he was thinking. You remember going out to the orchards at night, drinking, how you can see the stars all out? It's pretty when you're with other people, but when you're by yourself . . . And Oklahoma's flat. Flat, flat—flatter than here."

"He didn't kill himself, did he?" I ask him, because the way he's talking is making me nervous, the anticipation of terrible news.

"Nah, he didn't," Brother John says, pursing his lips. "We went on like that for a long time. A long time. Then one day I came home from school and Gary's things were gone—his clothes, even the bed. He left me a note taped to the mirror in the bathroom, explaining how it wasn't right, saying he went back to South Carolina. Back to his little town."

This is where the tears start, and the waiter comes by as if he's been listening the whole time. "Everything all right?" he asks. He must be sixteen or seventeen, young, and he looks like one of the Ochoa brothers.

"Some bad news is all," I tell him, and Brother John holds his head in his hands, and I'm grateful that the waiter walks away before Brother John begins again.

"I loved Gary. I really did. And I ran out of money and couldn't concentrate on the studying anymore, so I just came back home," he says, sobbing softly, and if only it weren't here in this restaurant, I would listen. But it's difficult. "It's been real hard to keep inside, ever since I came back. But I don't have anywhere else to go. I don't have family. I only had him. And I remember telling myself, all those times walking home from the bar in that little town, *This is it, this is it.* How could he go like that? I just couldn't believe it when I read that note, and I haven't heard from him since."

The waiter comes back with a coffeepot and two cups, even though we didn't ask for it. I'm too speechless to refuse him, and Brother John is too busy wiping away his tears, so the cups come down, and this means more that I have to sit through, waiting for the coffee to cool down, waiting for the check.

"For the longest time, I thought about going to South Carolina, to his little town, to find him. Call him out in the street in front of all his people and ask him why. But then I think about somebody doing that to me here and I know it would just be mean. At least he didn't kill himself, I hope."

I pour some sugar into my coffee, some of the warm milk, and slide the little condiment tray over to Brother John. He takes it calmly, the story out of him, and I figure maybe what he wants is a story in exchange. He wants to know about Over There, what you do when you feel like this Over There, where there isn't an empty wheat field to cry in. So I tell him a little bit, just to say something. But I just talk circles. I say that Over There is tall buildings. Over There is restaurants and the people who eat in them. I say that Over There is long, high windows by clean dining tables, and bright candles for the patrons. Over There is side streets with doors always open to the restaurant kitchens, the cooks sitting on the steps to get air. How there are enough restaurants Over There to employ actors and dancers who bend like Ls over the tables, enough work for the Mexican busboys and the dishwashers, how they all split the tips between cigarettes at the end of the long shift. Living Over There is cars and taxis, vans and too many horns, a bus to get you from one side of the city to the other whenever you needed.

I don't offer much more, and Brother John sips his coffee, quiet, not asking for more. What city doesn't have those things — tall buildings, too many cars, immigrants in the kitchen, actors and dancers eager for the spotlight? His face is done crying and it settles into resignation — he doesn't bother looking me in the eye.

The waiter brings the check, and both of us reach for our wallets. I don't want to do the dance of who pays, so I let Brother John put the money down when he insists and get up to leave. We walk out to the car, past families going in to eat, the smell of the brand-new tar of the parking lot in the air. When he shuts the car door, before I turn the ignition, Brother John clears his throat. He wants to revive the life in himself, and he says, "I loved that guy. Gary Lee Brown. I still love him . . . ," but I interrupt him.

"No more," I say apologetically. And then, "Keep it to yourself."

DURING THE REST OF the week, I think about Brother John next door, and I feel bad about how I left things with him. I nurse my aching hamstring in the quiet of the house, all of my nephews outside playing basketball, tireless. They'll come in filthy later, and it takes a long time to get all of them to wash their hands. I am lying on the couch and I close my eyes, hoping they'll stay out there until my brothers and sisters come back to collect them.

I keep wondering if I did the right thing by not telling Brother John my story, even though I knew he wanted to hear it. But I learned a long time ago to keep things simple. Don't tell much. Don't tell everything. Don't reveal what people don't need or want to know. It makes it easier all around.

Of my father: say no more of what happened to end the marriage. Of my brothers and sisters: nothing of the spider-cracks in their own unions. Of my tía Carolina: nothing of the money she stole from her job as the cashier of the mini-mart. Look at the people we went to school with: Agustina, though she knew the father of her baby, never brought him up. Ginger, whose mother worked with the school superintendent, wore big sweaters to hide the pregnancy. Maybe credit should have gone, then, to Ginger's mother for saving reputations all around. Beto and Carla married at the Iglesia de San Pedro, and no one raised a fuss, not even Patsy, alone and with no kids to show for her time with Beto. Violeta never talks about what is wrong with her insides, never takes her older sister Sofía's tragedy and brings it under the wing of her own misery. Emilio never admits that the accident at the paper mill might have been his fault, might have been caused by the sips of whiskey and the pot during his long breaks at four in the morning. *No one needs to know the whole story*, I wish I could tell Brother John. No one wants to know what Lily does in her car while she waits outside the houses of the men she loves. No one wants to know about Gary Lee Brown.

But I can't explain it to Brother John without telling him about the Actor. Take the Actor: when the Actor told me he was an actor, I had wanted to know what kind, because *actor* didn't differentiate him from any of the other actors Over There — stage actors, musical theater actors, dancers who did some acting because there were more opportunities to act than to dance, improv players, experimental and fringe performers, porn stars, soap actors, commercial hounds, film extras. But it had become apparent that I didn't need to know. All that I needed to know was the Actor's last hour at the bar, that the flirtations with the customers were nothing more than a way to get bigger tips, and that neither of us had to admit that this would be nothing more than a few brief months of small arguments and jealousies, caught hours and inconsequence. There would be no telling each other where we grew up and who our last boyfriend was and why it didn't work out. I learned to keep it to sitting at the bar, having two drinks, watching the Actor bend elegantly down, watching the customers admire that elegance. For all his story, Brother John got nothing; I left out my part about the Actor, about dating the Actor, then loving him, sitting at the bar and waiting for the end of his shift, watching as he stretched over a table to deliver drinks, a sharp L as the customers peered up at him.

"You shouldn't go on the plane like that, hurt and everything," my father says. His voice surprises me, and I open my eyes to see him standing over the couch. "Why don't you stay until you get better?"

"I have only a couple of vacation days," I tell him. "I have to go back." I put my hand over my eyes, as if I have a headache, but really it's to ward him off. We have not had our usual session of just the two of us sitting in a room, quiet, until he asks the questions that still eat away at him, the questions about my mother. Each and every time, I refuse to answer. I stay quiet and let him ponder on his own because I don't know how to relieve his exasperation.

"Why are you Over There anyway?" my father asks me.

"Dad, lay off," I say, sighing, and I rub my hamstring as if he's irritating it. My hand is still over my eyes, but I don't have to look at him to realize that our usual session is here, the two of us quiet. I think about the difficulty of easing anyone's pain after a sudden departure, the lack of reasons, the loss of hope. I can see Brother John in a small room in the wide plains of Oklahoma, the weather battering the thin glass of the windows of his attic apartment, him standing there and trying to ease his own confusion. It makes it easier to picture my father in this house on the first night after my mother's departure, how Brother John's story has allowed me to imagine. But then I realize my father has let go of those questions and those hurts, at least temporarily.

After a long while, I speak. "Dad," I ask, "why did you send me over to Brother John?" I keep my hand over my eyes, my other hand rubbing at my hamstring.

He does not answer. He stands at the foot of the couch. I can hear the clock ticking above the television set, the boys outside arguing, the ball bouncing against the dirt driveway. I still have my hand over my eyes, blind to my father's reaction, and the longer he stays silent, the more I want the pain in my leg to stay fiery and fierce, my hand over my eyes like a blindfold.

IDA Y VUELTA

JOAQUÍN'S VOICE TOLD HIM over the phone that he was returning because of his father's cancer, and as soon as Roberto heard the word, he knew what it meant: Joaquín's father was already in the hospital and near the end. It was that way around here, how the old people kept their pains hidden until it was too late. The discovery of their afflictions was always too late, always meant an end was coming. Roberto listened to Joaquín's tired voice tell him about driving back to the Valley on Friday after work. He lived in Menlo Park these days, over in the Bay Area, and he'd been gone for what seemed a long time to Roberto, though it had only been a year.

"How long are you staying?" Roberto asked him. It was Wednesday evening and November.

"I don't think it'll be more than a few days," Joaquín answered, and his voice suggested that relatives were being summoned home, the older ones coming by car all the way from Texas. Some were probably keeping watch already at the hospital in nearby Visalia, fifteen miles away. Their town had shut down its own hospital years ago; where Roberto lived, on the south side of town, he'd sometimes hear the sirens wailing, ambulances rushing all that way to Visalia, and he imagined some never made it.

"I'm really sorry to hear that," Roberto said. "I didn't know your dad was sick."

"He didn't either," Joaquín said. "Well, no, he did — he must have. I looked up all this info on colon cancer, and he must have been shitting black for months already."

Roberto didn't know what to say to that, but Joaquín cleared his throat, the way he always did when he needed to ask a favor.

"I can't stay at my house," Joaquín told him. "I'm bringing him with me."

"Oh."

"I just wanted to let you know. He wanted to come along. You know, because it's important . . ."

"No, of course, please," Roberto stammered. To see him, after a year — there would be no other way out, and he held back his hesitation and his jealousy.

"Friday night, then," Joaquín said, his voice level and satisfied. After they exchanged quick, swallowed good-byes, Roberto set about cleaning the apartment, dusting and wiping down the counters, emptying the drainboard of its clean dishes, tossing the junk mail he'd let languish for weeks. He ran the vacuum over the living room carpet, even though it was evening and the couple next door might be watching television. But this was where they would sleep, Joaquín and the new boyfriend from Menlo Park, here on the floor in a nest of blankets and thick pillows from the couch. There had been a time when Joaquín was hurting, Roberto had to remind himself, to resist the anger that was building up inside him — the stories Joaquín had told of crossing over into the United States when he was young, the scorching desert sands of Arizona and cupping stagnant water from a trough to keep himself alive. But that was a different kind of pain, an unfair comparison; still, it was all Roberto could think of to ward off the jealousy. A year ago, it was he whom Joaquín had folded into, as if acting in a dream, his dark brown arms involuntary, Roberto awake at night and running his fingers over the deep, circular scar on Joaquín's left arm, from his immunization back in Mexico. Or finding the line of three birthmarks on the left side of his belly by memory in the darkness of the bedroom.

Roberto rose early on Thursday morning, pulling the blinds of his kitchen window all the way up to the top. The view opened out on the spare, grassless backyard and high fence, which still couldn't blot out the horizon of peach orchards and walnut groves. This was what came of the south side of town's expanding, eating up the farmland, the field lizards still confused as they scampered around in the dust. He made a full pot of coffee, time still to relax before going to work, and watched the sun burn off the dew from the fence, the steam barely perceptible as the wood soaked up the morning warmth. Had Joaquín heard about the way the town had changed since he had left? Would his parents have bothered to tell him? And even if they had mentioned that Roberto lived in the new apartment complex over there just south of Kamm Avenue, where an old nectarine grove used to be, there was no way for them to know that the complex remained half-empty because it was too expensive for the town, the windows dark at dusk, and how Roberto could hear the rustle of the orchard leaves at night even with the window closed. They were slowly going gold for autumn.

After a stretch of hot sand, a trough of stagnant water, it's easy to leave a world behind. Ever since Joaquín had told him those desert stories, Roberto took them as his own, walking the steps in his imagination: boredom was nothing to face down, and he understood how easy it was for Joaquín, after all their time together, to admit that he was restless and maybe even out of love and that the answer seemed to be in a bigger city, despite his having no savings, no job set, and no family close by. Those weren't true obstacles, and if they were, Joaquín reasoned, they wouldn't be in the way very long. Roberto thought of this as he got into his car to make the short drive to the convalescent home in Kingsburg, where he worked soothing the tender backs of elderly patients, calming them in Spanish. Fifteen years now. Complacency or good reasoning, he couldn't tell which had kept him suited in the pristine white uniform and vinyl shoes for a steady paycheck. "I don't want you to come with me," Joaquín had said. "Because I can only take care of myself."

All day at work, Roberto listened to the pained sighs of relief his hands brought, concentrating on those sounds. When he first started at the convalescent home, his hands shook terribly; he was terrified that he was handling the patients too roughly. Now he understood the moans, the phlegm-coated pleadings caught in the throats of the old white ladies, the old Mexican señores with their faces stern through the indignity of another man's touching them. Roberto listened today as Señor Félix Vardo closed his eyes and sighed with resignation, allowed himself to be heaved over on his side, Roberto's hands manipulating the skin, circulating the blood back there. Today, Señora Susana de la Monte actually smiled, able to lift her own feet onto the pillow for Roberto to work on the swelling, and she thanked him even though he was far from being done. As with all the other patients, he massaged her hands afterward, lathering generously with his own store-bought lotion, and as Señora de la Monte's eyes met his in silent appreciation, Roberto thought of Joaquín's father. Sometimes the nurses at the front desk would clue him in on the status of a particular patient, usually on arrival or departure, and show him the telltale darkness creeping into the X-rays sent over by the radiologists. The patients never seemed to know why they had arrived or why they were departing — their families signed the papers, their faces blank expressions of exhaustion — but

Roberto knew. He thought of Joaquín's father in the Visalia hospital, and he knew.

Out on the loading dock at lunchtime, he offered his supervisor a cigarette before she had time to take out her own pack. "Trudy," he said, lighting her cigarette, "do you mind if I work a double tonight? Get off for Friday?"

"You look tired already," Trudy told him. She was a grossly fat woman with blond hair cut close to her neck, tiny glasses perched on her nose. Although everyone liked her, it was widely known that she had become manager because her weight prevented her from doing any of the more strenuous work. But she was a kind person and good with numbers.

"I have people coming tomorrow," Roberto said. "I just found out."

"Family?" Trudy asked, coughing. "They staying with you?"

"You know how it is."

"Sure," she said. "I'll pull someone off for tonight. There's always somebody who'd rather work daytime."

"Thanks," he told her, though he could feel himself tiring already at the thought of not leaving until one in the morning.

"I can't give you overtime, though," Trudy pointed out. "Late notice. They'll get on me if you raise a stink, so that's the only condition."

"Fine," Roberto said, nodding. "Fine." He finished his cigarette and waited silently for Trudy, not rushing her. For November, the afternoon was warm, almost eighty degrees, but when night came, the temperature would plummet, the open Valley sky snatching away all the heat. He would be fast asleep, though, too tired to pace around as he usually did when anxiety gripped him too hard. This evening, after most of the patients would have been urged to sleep for the night, Roberto planned to walk the floors anyway, engage the few who tossed and turned, peeked through doors to investigate the hallways, stumbled about. He planned to volunteer himself for the harder work in the kitchen, stowing away dishes and the heavy food trays. All of this to drive home tired at one in the morning and collapse into bed, oblivious and not needing to face the quiet hours.

WHEN ROBERTO WOKE AT two on Friday afternoon, the November light was angling low into his bedroom, the daytime nearly done. He sat on the edge of the bed with a sense of relief. The night hours had come and gone, the stretch of being trapped by the quiet streets, the hush over the apartment complex, with nowhere to go for solace. He hated those times, those hours of darkness when he could not sleep. With the afternoon light it was easier for his heart to juggle around all the old questions grinding into him like broken glass. It soothed him to hear the faint patter of the couple next door washing dishes in their kitchen sink, the tick of heels on the walkway in front of his apartment.

He heard his cell phone ring and he stumbled into the living room to retrieve it. It was Joaquín.

"I'm parked next to your car," Joaquín said. "Which one's your apartment?"

"You're here already?" Roberto asked groggily. He walked

over to the front door and opened it, stretched out to see the far
end of the complex, where the parking lot was, and there was
Joaquín, waving.

Roberto watched him as he put the cell phone in his pocket
and leaned into the red Datsun pickup to pull out a duffel bag.
Joaquín was talking to someone in the passenger seat, as if coaxing him out. The other door opened, and Roberto stood watching, still shirtless and wearing his boxer shorts, suddenly aware of
the twenty-five pounds he'd put on since last year. He could see
the other figure emerge, smaller than Joaquín, probably younger,
and as the two of them headed in the direction of the apartment,
Roberto ducked back inside to put on some clothes.

"Hi," Joaquín greeted him, nudging the front door open with
his duffel bag. He motioned the boyfriend in with an assuring nod
of his head. "This is Robbie," he said to Roberto. "Robbie, this
is my friend Roberto."

Robbie stepped into the apartment holding his own duffel bag,
extending his hand to Roberto. He was a good ten, if not fifteen,
years younger, maybe in his early twenties, and his green eyes
set Roberto to guessing about his background, his people. It disappointed Roberto to see someone so different from the person
he had imagined. He had expected to see a mirror of himself,
someone to project some jealousy upon, someone whose look and
manner would prove that Joaquín might have given him up but
was still seeking someone just like him. Instead, Robbie had the
edge of the city about him. The dark brown shirt he wore was
perfectly fitted, the short sleeves tucked around little mounds of

biceps, streaks of orange running up the side of the fabric in the shape of an hourglass. It would be impossible to find a shirt like that here. "Good to meet you," he said, shaking Robbie's hand and looking at the green eyes, which were gigantic, hopeful and innocent, and somehow manipulative. "We're tocayos."

"He means you're the same, like twins," Joaquín told Robbie, who looked perplexed. "Because you have the same name."

"But my name's Robbie."

"You don't speak Spanish?" Roberto asked him.

"No," Robbie answered. "I was born here."

"So was I."

Joaquín almost seemed to step between them. "I lied at work," he said. "I called in sick."

"Me, too," Robbie said.

"What do you do?"

"I cut hair," Robbie answered, snipping his fingers in the air to demonstrate. "That's how I met him."

"Oh yeah?"

"I bet him along the way that you called in sick, too," Joaquín said quickly. "And I was right."

"Actually, I took a double last night."

"That's just like you." Joaquín unzipped the duffel bag and pawed through it. "I need to shower and then get over to the hospital." He pointed down the hall and began walking that way. "Bathroom?"

Roberto nodded.

"It's a nice apartment," Robbie said, sitting on the couch.

"For this area, yeah." Roberto could hear vigorous splashing in the bathroom. Joaquín was in a hurry, whether to get to the hospital or to keep him from talking to Robbie, he wasn't sure. "How long have you been dating him?"

"It'll be a year around Christmas."

"Is that right?"

"He'd come in a couple of times already, and he would always leave me a nice tip. And he would sleep in the chair during his cut."

"Christmas? That's a lot of haircuts in a month. He only left in November." Roberto could almost see Joaquín in the chair of Robbie's shop, hair wet and combed down, Robbie's fingers delicate around his ears, the snip of the scissors and the click of the metal against the comb. It was easy to imagine Joaquín's eyes opening and meeting Robbie's in the mirror as Robbie judged his work, then closing again; and as Roberto stood there imagining this, he let go of the chance to ask Robbie the basic questions—how old was he, and where was he from, and where did he get those green eyes? By that time, Joaquín had emerged from his hurried shower, towel wrapped around his waist, and even the familiarity of his body, the inoculation scar on his left arm visible all over again, did not break Roberto from his thinking.

"Go shower," Joaquín said, taking the duffel bag and walking to Roberto's bedroom to put on fresh clothes, but Robbie declined. "Change, then," he called out. "Put on something respectable."

Robbie raised his eyebrows and pulled at the hem of his shirt, looking over at Roberto for silent affirmation.

"You've never met his people, have you?"

• • •

PEOPLE WILL FORGIVE ANYTHING if you help them. But it depends on the people. Joaquín's people — he had a lot of them in the Valley, both immediate family and friends from his pueblito in Jalisco — always gave Roberto a feeling of being graced and redeemed for his basic decency. Roberto, after all, was the one who enrolled Joaquín in high school all those years ago when they were neighbors on Gold Street. Roberto the one who straightened out Joaquín's legal tangles with Immigration and the one who managed to find him a construction job out of high school. They had Roberto to thank for Joaquín's English, the wiping out of the accent over the years — he could have been born here. What Joaquín's people had in Roberto was a translator, a person to open the government envelopes and make the calls, a filer for their taxes, a negotiator to get a distant cousin into the States safely, a way to put money in the bank instead of hiding it in the house. When, in their twenties, Roberto and Joaquín moved in together, Joaquín's people kept silent, though Roberto knew it offended them deeply. It was best to ignore their discomfort, like the cancer lurking deep inside Joaquín's father, and hope instead that such a malignancy would devour itself; but the years just kept going, until there came a point, finally, when Joaquín's people found Roberto's services a fair exchange for the shame.

The day after Joaquín announced he was leaving him, Roberto had been due at Joaquín's parents' home to explain an important letter they had received from their car insurance company. It was a one-page letter, and he had not needed more than a minute or two to read that the company wanted to sever the policy because of a recent fender bender, but Joaquín's parents had made Roberto sit down at the vinyl-covered kitchen table and Joaquín's mother had brought him a cup of manzanilla tea and a piece of Mexican bread.

"I knew a woman once who married a man from Mexico," Joaquín's father had told him in Spanish, rubbing the brim of the cowboy hat that he always wore. "Married him and worked a good job, helped him with his papers, and even raised all four of his kids. And don't you know that this man took up with another woman, right over there in Fowler? Divorced the woman who helped him and his kids—all that money, all that time." Joaquín's mother shook her head, listening, remembering, and Roberto marveled at her easy agreement. He knew what she had taken, what she had endured from Joaquín's father, and yet she listened on from the secure place of a marriage held together by will.

"A real shame," Joaquín's father told him, "when people don't have an ounce of decency. I want to tell you how much my son shames us for what he's done to you."

Joaquín's mother kept nodding in agreement, and when Roberto met her eyes, he felt that maybe he had misunderstood the enormity of Joaquín's leaving, his departure, and that Joaquín's parents knew what it signified better than he. Joaquín's mother alone, perhaps, knew why love mattered, even if it meant loving the wrong person, and she looked at Roberto with extraordinary, unexpected empathy. Both of Joaquín's parents knew about distances and crossing those gaps, about the hours of worry, and the reconciliations in the middle of the night, knew that there would be no return. They knew how people came and went, sometimes arriving, sometimes not.

"I'm always going to help you," Roberto had assured them, dropping his eyes to the paper, and when he had to tell them the bad news about the car insurance, they took it well. He had known, though, that from then on they would always have trouble asking him for assistance.

NOT FORTY MINUTES AFTER they left, after Robbie had fussed with the ironing of a long-sleeved blue shirt with a delicate diamond pattern, Roberto heard the phone ring. "Could you come get him at the hospital? My mom made a big stink."

"What happened?" Roberto asked. "Just send him home in the Datsun. He won't get lost."

"He can't drive stick," Joaquín explained. "And my dad is real sick, so I can't leave. You should have seen my mom go off on me when I brought him in there. Everyone yelling, and the nurses came over to see what all the noise was about."

Roberto sighed. "Well, you knew better."

"My dad's out, completely out. And my mom points at him and says, 'He can hear everything you're saying. You think he doesn't know what you're doing?'"

"Fine," Roberto said. "I'll come pick him up. Tell him to wait outside so I don't have to park."

On the other end of the line, he could almost hear Joaquín hesitate, swallow, close his eyes. Finally, before hanging up, Joaquín said, "Thanks. Really. I'm sorry."

"I'll be there in twenty, okay? Tell him what kind of car I drive."

When he arrived, Roberto could spot the brightness of Robbie's shirt from the very end of the parking lot, radiant against the shade of the long archway leading to the hospital's front entrance. He beeped the horn, and Robbie turned to the car as if in surprise—if he had been searching for Roberto's car, he hadn't been very alert, probably drifting off, Roberto thought, into his anger with Joaquín. He could see the scowl on Robbie's face as he made his way to the car, and when Robbie got in, he slammed the door.

"This isn't the Datsun," Roberto told him, easing forward to the street.

"Sorry," Robbie said, then added, a little less curtly, "I didn't mean to do that."

"You know, it isn't any of my business, but maybe I should have said something before you went along. I thought it was a bad idea."

"Well, they liked you."

"I lived with him for almost fifteen years. There's a big difference."

Roberto drove to the new pass-through on Highway 198, a clear shot along the north stretch of Visalia, and soon they were back out on the country road headed to town. It was hot, like the day before, which was unusual for November; across one of the empty cotton fields, a dust devil swirled lazily, meandering. "Look at that," Roberto said.

"I've never seen one. It's like a tornado."

"Harmless. It's just the heat. Don't they have fields where you grew up?"

"I grew up in Menlo Park. It's all houses."

"How old are you, Robbie?"

"I'm twenty-seven."

"That's young," Roberto said. "Too young for Joaquín, in my opinion."

"I'm mature for my age," Robbie said defensively. "And besides, he's been with me for almost a year already."

"I didn't say you weren't mature. I just said you're too young for Joaquín. There's a big difference."

"And what would that be?"

"Oh, about fifteen years."

Robbie fidgeted in his seat, as though eager to be somewhere else. But Roberto knew there was nowhere to go, not for miles, with the cotton fields surrounding them and the county landfill and the dairy barns with the cows idling at the roadside fences. Just the miles sailing endlessly on the straight road, not even a stop sign where Robbie could hop out of the car dramatically and insist on walking back to town.

"You know, I really wanted to meet you," Robbie finally offered. "Joaquín talks a lot about you, says a lot of good things. He thought you wouldn't have a problem with this."

"With what? With him dating you?" Roberto shrugged.

"I thought you'd be nicer about it, just because of how he talks about you, I mean."

"Look, that was a whole year ago," he said, sighing. "He's his own person and he'd been bored with his life here for a long time, just frustrated, and that was that. I don't blame myself anymore. People come and go."

"I would be more angry about it. More bitter. After all those years of being with him, it doesn't matter to you? I just can't believe it. I get all messed up when we argue, thinking he's going to leave me."

"He's not going to leave you," Roberto said. "Not if you keep wanting him." He stared out at the approaching line of nectarine groves, acres of them continuing all the way up to his very bedroom window. The groves seemed to take forever to arrive, the car moving so slowly. The space between them went slack with silence. Out of the corner of his eye, in the quick glances in the rearview mirror to check the diesel truck behind them, Roberto could see Robbie as he sat motionless, uncertain. Something in the discomfort thrilled Roberto, the feeling that he had the upper hand over Robbie, that he understood his want and the kind of love he had for Joaquín, something at once stupid and tender. Still, he wasn't proud of this manipulation, and he knew that Robbie deserved none of his scorn. None of this, after all, was his fault.

"You just deserve better," Roberto said, breaking the silence in the car, but it only parted the air like the dust devil on the cotton field, riding through, everything settling right back down where it had been, the moment descending, spiraling some, but ultimately vanishing.

They would have hours ahead of them, until nightfall at least, when Joaquín would return, and as Roberto pulled into the parking lot of the apartment complex, he debated going off to the grocery store without Robbie. Robbie got out of the car and closed the door almost apologetically, hands in his pockets, and walked behind Roberto as they made their way to his apartment. Roberto jingled the keys, wanting the noise to hide his nervousness, and debated how the excuse to go to the store would sound. He let them into the apartment, then walked over to the kitchen to open up a cabinet and declare something lacking for dinner, but when he turned around to say it, Robbie had come up behind him, his steps quiet, and his green eyes were looking up at him. Robbie leaned closer to him and tilted his head up to kiss him. There was nothing passionate about it, just the flesh of their lips touching, both of them with their eyes open, Roberto wanting to see Robbie's green eyes and not knowing why Robbie kept them open. It was when Robbie closed his eyes to him, shut away the green, that the kiss became deeper, wetter, and Robbie's tongue began searching. Roberto allowed himself to touch him, just the arms first, through the soft fabric of the blue shirt, the stitching of the delicate diamond pattern, and the small biceps beneath. Robbie's hands reached down to feel if Roberto was hard, and Roberto closed his eyes finally because he wasn't. He ignored the self-conscious tightening of his own back when Robbie ran his hands up his shirt, discovering the layer of fat around his middle, but Robbie's hands glided over it. He kept his eyes closed and imagined how it was for Joaquín to feel this, the patch of hair on Robbie's belly and the smooth skin up above, the shirt that unfastened with clasps and not buttons, the tiny, hard nipples. And though Robbie had none of Joaquín's height or thickness of torso or wide shoulders, Roberto kissed as if remembering him, knowing that Robbie's skin was what Joaquín touched with light fingers, that it somehow contained Joaquín, at least if Roberto just kept his eyes closed.

Robbie stopped and stared up at him. They stood in the silence of the kitchen, and Robbie would not break away from Roberto's line of sight, would not blink. Robbie reached down again to feel if Roberto was hard, and when he discovered that he was, he led Roberto with his other hand in the direction of the bedroom, and there, finally, they broke their hold on each other. Roberto's hands shook as he closed the blinds against the afternoon sun, as he took off his clothes, watching Robbie do the same. His hands could not stop shaking as he thought of what he was doing, of Joaquín's parents in the hospital only fifteen miles away, of his own empty, lonely months, of the reasons why Robbie was doing this. Neither one of them would speak, and they fumbled awkwardly on the bed, limbs getting in the way, the bed squeaking from their weight. After a while, Robbie positioned himself underneath and looked at him expectantly, and it shamed Roberto to admit that he had no condoms in the apartment, all the months he had gone without — first the months after Joaquín left, then the months when he could do nothing but remember. He shook his head at Robbie. "I don't have any . . ."

Robbie seemed to contemplate the situation for a moment,

saying nothing. For a long time, he looked into Roberto's eyes without blinking, running his fingers against his back, as if coaxing him. Then almost imperceptibly, his legs loosened their grip around Roberto's waist and slowly his knees straightened back down to meet the mattress. It would be wrong to try to kiss him, Roberto knew, so after a moment he rose from the bed, as if to free Robbie from his own trap, and shyly put his clothes back on.

"Will you come to the store with me?" he asked Robbie, clearing his throat, and he was somewhat surprised when Robbie agreed.

THE STORY WENT THAT Joaquín's mother still loved Joaquín's father even after he had had the affair. The story went that she sat at the kitchen table with the lights out, save for the glow of a cigarette. She had never smoked before. But she loved him and she had waited. When was that — back when it was just she and her husband alone in the States, back when Joaquín himself was but a baby and still being bathed with creek water in that village in Mexico? It's easy to forgive when pride is obliterated, ignored, made to dissolve into nothing with a pull on the cord for the lightbulb in the kitchen. It's easy to forgive, easy as stubbing out the cigarette in a little blue dish with green roses in the center, washing it with hot water and soap, and putting it away. It's easy to love the wrong person, even after much time has passed since the sudden discovery of betrayal. It's as easy as holding the hand of the dying man and giving thanks that it is happening in a hospital in Visalia, California, and not in the rusted heavy bed back in Jalisco. It's easy to pretend there never was that white woman with four kids of her own, that woman who still lives in the town, easy to pretend she has stopped existing.

It's easy to forgive, but it's hard to understand it. It's hard to understand how anyone can pretend, how love trumps reason and understanding. In that wing of the hospital, slouched in the aquamarine couches, arms crossed, dozing, Joaquín's family had been waiting through the hours, when, near eight o'clock, toward the end of official visiting time, the news was whispered quietly to one of the men and his lowered hat answered everyone's pleadings. Who was to say who loved him more, who forgave him more, who had more to forgive? The wailing came in floods, the arms in the air grasping, the shoulders shuddering. Who was to say which uncle would drink the most later that night, and who was to say what he would be trying to hide in such sorrow? Whose hand was held longest, hardest, in those final hours, the old man's bony wrists against the crisp, folded-down creases of the hospital's bedsheets? Who was to say what the old man was trying to say, one of the last sounds he made, a word trapped in his mouth like a fly buzzing, that sound he made when Joaquín, of all people, held his hand and announced himself present?

There was an enormous amount of food on the table, plates half-wrapped in plastic, and Joaquín ate hungrily. It was near midnight when he returned from Visalia, unannounced, because Robbie found him impossible to reach on the cell phone. Earlier that afternoon, Roberto had led the way through the grocery store, looking for items that required work, to lull the uncomfortable hours away: green beans with their ends to be snapped, swirled around with tomato and onion; ground beef for albóndiga soup, and a bag of rice to roll into the meatballs; a flan mix that required setting. All afternoon, he and Robbie chopped vegetables, watched rice soften, stirred soup, both of them listening for Joaquín's tired entry at the front door. But the evening set in; they both ate quietly at the table and then cleaned up the kitchen, leaving it spotless.

"My mother says he waited for me," Joaquín said, rolling a corn tortilla and dipping it into the albóndiga soup.

"You don't believe her? People do that, you know." Roberto unwrapped the green beans and pointed to them, encouraging. "I see it at the convalescent home. They can hang on if they know someone's coming."

"I don't believe in that," Joaquín answered, picking at the green beans. "You made all this?"

"I helped," Robbie said.

"He wasn't alert even." Joaquín motioned around his head with both hands, rolled tortilla still in one, parting the air around him as if it were fog. "What could he understand at that point? What could he know?"

"They can hear what's happening," Roberto assured him.

"You sound like my mother," Joaquín said. "And no, they can't."

Roberto and Robbie sat at the table, watching Joaquín devour the food, and when he finished the bowl of soup, he looked expectantly at Robbie, who rose to ladle more and reheat it in the microwave. Roberto watched him go, so dutiful, Joaquín picking at the green beans and having a spoonful of rice at the same time. There was something wrong with this need to fill his hunger after what he had seen.

"When's the funeral?" Robbie asked, setting the bowl down gently.

"Thursday is what my uncle said. But I'm not sticking around that long."

"What?" Roberto asked, incredulous. "You've got to be kidding . . ." He was stunned by Joaquín's complete lack of compassion, his rush to move past the family obligation. It struck Roberto as cruel, unforgivable. But this was part of his nature, the way Joaquín had always been, and Roberto found himself keeping his criticism to himself as he had always done over the years, allowing Joaquín the open road to pursue whatever he craved. Joaquín's mother—her eyes that day when Joaquín's father had hypocritically denounced him—rattled voiceless in his head. She nodded at Roberto in memory, speechless, as if she understood how he could have loved someone like Joaquín to begin with.

"Hey, I've got a job. I've got bills to pay," Joaquín said, raising his voice. "I'm not sticking around all week. For what? So my drunk uncles can come around asking to borrow money for a headstone?"

"Jesus . . ."

He waved Roberto quiet. "Really, just . . . just lay off." He continued eating, finishing the second bowl of albóndigas. Without a fresh spoon, without wiping off the one he used for the soup, he dipped into the flan. Dissatisfied, he ate only two bites.

Roberto rose to clean off the table, half-tempted to ask Joaquín to help him, but it would be no use. Joaquín would ignore him, and it was his own kitchen that would suffer in the end. "Robbie," he said, "there's some blankets in that hall closet. And pillows on the couch."

"We get the floor?" Joaquín asked.

He didn't answer him, pretending to be absorbed in settling the food back into the refrigerator. By the time he finished washing the dishes and turned away from the sink, both Joaquín and Robbie were on the floor, nestled in the blankets, and he turned off the lights without saying good night.

In bed, Roberto felt increasingly awake as the minutes wore on. Every time he closed his eyes, he had a new image to contend with, something to make him open up to the darkness again. If it wasn't the clasps on Robbie's shirt, it was the way his hair felt. And if it wasn't Robbie's hair, then it was Joaquín's mother being served tea laced with a powder provided by a neighbor woman, something to calm her nerves. Or he'd picture himself filling out forms for Joaquín's father, as if he had been at the convalescent home, and all the procedures they had to go through when a patient died. The orchard leaves rustled more loudly than usual, and then he could hear the patter of rain, the first of the season. He listened to it come down, not a hard rain, just enough to wake anyone in the lightest of sleeps, even Joaquín's mother despite her nerve-calming tea. A great shame filled him to think of her just then, lying in a bed that she had slept in alone for weeks now, while he thought of Robbie and Joaquín on the floor of his apartment. That white woman with the four kids, maybe she too had heard the news by now, awake and listening to the rain and remembering.

From down the hallway, from beyond the closed door of his bedroom, he heard a deep moan. It wasn't Joaquín. He listened for it, but he didn't hear it again. Only the rain. It saddened Roberto enough that sleep continued to refuse him. His heart broke for Joaquín's mother and her enduring such a man after so many years; in thinking of her, his heart broke for himself all over again, for having been just like her, the years wasted loving someone like that: you love someone because there might never be anyone else. He listened to the rain and thought of Joaquín's inoculation scar, Robbie's fingers knowing in the dark where the three birthmarks were and reaching out for them. Outside, he knew the rain would finally begin to empty the gold leaves from the trees.

WHEN HE WOKE IN the morning, Roberto found the blankets folded neatly on the couch. Had the duffel bags not been near the door, he would have thought Joaquín had left early and without saying good-bye. "Joaquín?" he called out stupidly, but the apartment was empty. The coffeepot was on and two cups were in the sink, unwashed. When he served himself a mug, he spotted the note. *I took him to church.* The coffee was terrible: he couldn't tell which of them had made it.

The Iglesia de San Pedro would hold a Saturday service twice this morning, but there was no telling how long Joaquín and Robbie had been gone. It was nearing eleven o'clock, the hour of the second service; perhaps they had gone to eat breakfast first. Roberto peeked outside the window. The sky held gray, but there were no heavy, dark clouds around, and overnight the rain had paused. It would be a day with little more than weak light.

Roberto looked down at the two duffel bags, both zipped and ready to go. He wondered why they hadn't loaded them onto the Datsun and been done with it, and then he quietly granted Joaquín the grace of trying to reassure him: he would return to say good-bye and to be sure there were no hard feelings. The person needing the most comfort right then, he knew, was Joaquín's mother, but he felt his loneliness stretching before him like a road, the mirage of water at the end of it wavering, beckoning him. Roberto looked down at the duffel bags, tempted to unzip them and rummage through, not looking for anything, but just to feel what was inside: the blue shirt with the delicate diamonds, if Robbie wasn't wearing it again, or the brown shirt with the orange on the sides. Or in Joaquín's bag, perhaps a shirt he remembered, the color, the feel. If he dipped his head to smell the interior of the bag, would he come up with the scent he still remembered from all those years?

He unzipped one of the bags, slowly and quietly, as if Joaquín and Robbie were in the next room. He listened for the sound of footsteps out on the walkway, but there was only the wind rattling through the bushes. Robbie's brown shirt was on top, the orange almost gleaming up at him. Roberto knelt on the floor and bent his head down, breathing in the scent of it deeply. *I love you*, he imagined Robbie saying to Joaquín the night before on the hard floor of his living room, and there was this scent for Joaquín to breathe in, a powdery citrus, very clean. *Te quiero tanto*, Joaquín's mother had said, all those years ago, when she turned on the kitchen light to forgive Joaquín's father. Roberto closed the bag and did not open the other one. He did not want to remember himself, like Joaquín's mother grasping her arms around her husband's neck, saying those same words just last year, trying to persuade Joaquín to stay.

All afternoon he waited. Saturday television had a few movies that he slept through, but still the door did not open. It began to rain by four o'clock, and it was only then that Joaquín and Robbie entered, both of them solemn, Joaquín's eyes red and swollen.

"It's time for us to head out," Joaquín said. "We just came to say good-bye."

"Are things okay?" Roberto asked, but Joaquín only shrugged. There was something larger to contend with, and he wanted to be on his way.

"It was good to meet you," Robbie said, his voice so quiet that it was a surprise to see his arm thrust out for a handshake.

"Likewise," he answered, and Robbie grabbed his duffel bag and hurried back out through the rain.

"Why don't you guys just wait out the storm?" Roberto asked. "Have you eaten?"

The way Joaquín stood, with that look in his eye, brought

Roberto back to last year and the broken promises. The empty feeling, too, of how Joaquín just drove away. In the days before Joaquín had left, Roberto had mentally rehearsed his departure, tried to have something final and absolute to tell him, but nothing had come, and he had been left imagining good-byes at midnight train stations, platforms filled with great blasts of steam, imagining the lonely blandness of an airport gate, an endless parking lot, a hallway so long he could stare forever at Joaquín's leaving and still Joaquín wouldn't turn back. It took a particular strength or denial—he couldn't tell which—to be that way. At the hospital the night before, when Joaquín's mother clutched her husband's hand and begged him to stay, Roberto knew who had let go first.

Joaquín picked up his duffel bag and hurried out onto the sidewalk. It was still raining, but not hard. "Wait," Roberto called out, running after him. He could see the silhouette of Robbie in the Datsun waiting, and he knew that if he hadn't called out, Joaquín would have gone down the walkway of the apartment complex and opened the truck door, the dome light like a star in the dim of the afternoon, but he wouldn't have turned around.

Roberto approached to hug him, and when his arms wrapped themselves around Joaquín's back, the familiarity came again, he thought, like Joaquín's mother reaching for the lightbulb in the kitchen, knowing where it was in the dark just by reaching out for it, and he said the words he knew he shouldn't.

Joaquín let go to leave. "I'll see you soon," he said.

SEÑOR X

L AS PALMAS IS THE only new building Gold Street has seen in years. On this side of town, there has not been much new construction in a long time. Over on the north side, the town is stretching its way toward Fresno, swallowing up farmland sold by farmers who claimed that the soil was too acidic. But that's a lie. The peaches, the nectarines, were growing just fine. Then one foggy day in January, I drove past the northern fringe of town and saw acres and acres of fruit trees pulled up, the trunks and branches gathered in piles. January: there were no leaves, no buds, just the bare dead trees, and as soon as the sun came to stay and the county waived air-quality restrictions for a few days, the farmers were allowed to burn their tree piles. That's greed for you: now there are beautiful, beautiful houses up there. Las Palmas, by comparison, isn't really that great. But since it's on this side of town, it's something else.

Las Palmas is two stories, like a good motel. My apartment is on the second floor and my bedroom window faces Treviño's backyard. Ever since I moved back to my neighborhood a few months ago, I've watched him out there. Like a lot of backyards in the neighborhood, it's full of junk: car parts, smashed aluminum cans for recycling, tire rims, old pieces of lumber. Junk has been back there for as long as I can remember. Treviño hunts through his treasures every day, moving slowly. Sometimes he inspects the cactus ridged against the fence and then produces a knife from his back pocket, slicing a heart for lunch. I remember him from when I was a kid and lived in my real house down the street, not in this apartment. Treviño's an old, old man now, but even with his wife dead many years, look at the things Treviño has: a lot of kids, even if only three of them come to visit him regularly; his own house, shoddy as it is; a perfectly restored Cadillac from the sixties, the envy of the entire neighborhood.

I've seen him drive his Cadillac, very slowly, as if he were king of the street. He always has the windows rolled down, and the neighborhood kids stop their playing to watch him go by. Treviño waves at them and they wave back, gathering to follow his car like a royal entourage. I used to wave at him, too. The black paint was and still is perfect, shiny and waxed, the taillights glimmering sharp even in the daylight.

Treviño's getting old, though: the Cadillac collects a little dust because he doesn't drive as much, and I know this makes him crazy. A neighborhood kid comes down the street every couple of days to wash it with rags and a bucket of soapy water. From the bedroom window, I can see Treviño supervising the kid, admonishing him, shaking his head, but he doesn't have much choice. I know it pains him to see his car lose out daily to the elements of the neighborhood. I know he stands there with his hands on his hips, shaking his head.

The thing is, I didn't think much about Treviño until one day when I was coming home from the store. As I parked my car in my slot, I noticed a little oil stain on the cement. My car was a brand-new used Tercel, and it was too soon to have a leak like that. Still, I unloaded my grocery bags and tried to pay it no mind. As I was walking toward the stairs leading up to my breezeway, the Mexican woman who had just moved in downstairs came out of her apartment in a rush, pulling her two little kids behind her. She was flustered, not enough hands to control the kids, who seemed to bolt down to the ground like dogs on a leash when they don't want to go any farther. In her struggle, the Mexican woman dropped some money, a fat little fold of bills, and my better side made me open my mouth and call out to her. "¡Oye, señora!" I pointed and she turned to look at me as if I didn't understand she was in a hurry. But when she spotted the money, her face washed over in relief. She bent over to pick it up and stuffed it past her blouse into the cup of her bra, gave a nod of thanks, and off they went, on foot, to wherever they were going.

I could have been a good neighbor. I could have offered her a ride, even if there was something wrong with my oil pump. I've been trying to change. I think I'm a good person deep inside, except for some mistakes, some ways of thinking that I now know were wrong. But I stood there watching the woman and her two kids on the long trudge to their destination, and I thought about her money, the fat little fold of bills.

And that's when it hit me: Las Palmas, this neighborhood, Treviño next door. People might be poor, but they were not destitute. They were savers. They shuttled money down to Mexico all the time. They distrusted the thieves at the banks. There was money everywhere in the neighborhood. But money to be made, not stolen. And then I thought of Treviño and his backyard, the work I might get out of him, and knew I needed to go over and introduce myself.

IT WAS A SATURDAY afternoon about four o'clock. I had dozed all day with the television on, sometimes going into my bedroom to see if Treviño had wandered into his backyard. Finally I saw him, and I watched him for a bit just to make sure he was going to stay outside for a while. Then I made my way over, knocked on his front door, pretended to wait, and then went along the side of the house to the backyard.

"Oye, Señor Treviño," I called out to him. He was hunched

over, bracing himself somehow against his right leg, pulling at a rusty piece of pipe trapped by two enormous fruit crates, the ones used for shipping oranges. Treviño turned around slowly, his face grimacing. I thought at first he was annoyed at having been interrupted, but then I realized he had lost his concentration, that it had been taking all his effort to get this piece of pipe. He was sweating a little through his plaid shirt, the same kind of thin, worn cotton shirt I always remembered him wearing. He looked at me almost with suspicion, but then that look flashed away, as if the old man had remembered the manners of his country, and he stood up as straight as he could and began walking over to me.

"Buenas tardes," Treviño said, wiping his hand on his khakis and extending it, even though we were still some distance apart. He greeted me as if I were familiar, so gracious, but I didn't know if he actually remembered me.

I pointed to the pipe and asked him, in Spanish, if he needed help.

"A little bit," Treviño answered, grinning slightly, and I wasn't sure if he was feeling sheepish about needing help or about his pronunciation. "You're one of the triplets, aren't you?" he asked.

I nodded at him.

"Well," he said, "which one are you?"

"Cristian. But I go by Chris."

"Your mama named you Cristian," he said, almost gruffly. "That's what you should go by."

I didn't think he was even going to give me a chance to ask

about helping out, but then he asked me about how I'd come to move back to Gold Street, and I told him about my new job at the paper mill on the north side of town. Treviño raised his eyes in surprise; he knew it was a good job, and maybe it made me sound like a man worth talking to. He forgot about the pipe and motioned me over to the shade near the back porch. Treviño took a lawn chair for himself and then pointed to my choices: a cinder block or an old fruit crate. I chose the crate and sat down.

I didn't have to ask him to start his story. "Sonora," he said. "All my people." And then the brothers over in Texas, the three daughters who still came to visit him from nearby Visalia. For the wife, almost ten years now since she had passed away. "I miss her every day," Treviño told me, looking away to the expanse of his backyard.

"She was a nice lady," I said. I really did remember her. I followed Treviño's eyes as he focused on an oil drum rusted on the sides and black on the rim from an old fire. He had weeds sprouting along the sagging wooden fences, the weeds already yellowed, the ground dry and dusty. He had an old swamp cooler, the kind some people still used in the summers here, the old box kind with a cylinder fan and a tray of water pooling at the bottom and the soft pads on the side, kept wet by a hookup to an outside faucet. Metal scraps curled up and ready for a good hammer; newspaper stacks in clear plastic to keep them safe from the rain; old coffee cans with their plastic lids still on, heavy with rusty nails.

"You ever think about cleaning up back here?" I asked him, swallowing a little. "Sell some of the scrap?"

"Who would want all this junk?" Treviño asked, laughing, but I knew he was waiting for the answer.

I had it all ready on the tip of my tongue. "A lot of people. Couple of dollars here and there. Probably the same people who would buy your Cadillac if you offered it for sale."

Treviño sighed and surveyed his treasures. Was he adding up the dollars in his head? Or was he imagining how his backyard might actually look if cleared of everything? He shifted in his lawn chair, the aluminum groaning. He tugged at the cuffs of his plaid shirt, the worn threads, then studied them closely as if I weren't there anymore.

"Back when my wife was alive, all this" — he waved with his hand — "full of grass, flowers all along the fence. Not just roses and petunias, but the fancy flowers like the white ladies. She used to have them in the front yard, but people would steal them. Can you believe it? Some of the neighborhood women lost a good friend in her by doing that."

"I'll bet it was nice," I told him, but I couldn't imagine it. I couldn't recall the backyard ever having looked like that.

Treviño clapped his hands, his decision made. "You over in Las Palmas, then? You need work?" He lit a cigarette and coughed, shaking his head as if he knew he shouldn't be doing it anymore.

"I've been looking for work. I'm only part-time at the mill."

"You know cars? There's a lot of good spare parts back here that will get good money, but you have to know car parts."

"Yeah, I know cars some," I lied. "All that scrap metal, even that newspaper. You can get something for that."

Treviño was still looking over his yard, looking at one corner, then another. He puffed on his cigarette with that resigned look of longing that comes with exhaling. Then he said it: "Flowers would look pretty again. A garden." Treviño shook his head as if at a memory. "You can start with that pipe," he said, pointing. "Somebody said they'd give me five bucks for it."

LAS PALMAS IS FOR people like that Mexican woman with her two kids. It's for young mothers on WIC. Old ladies live on the bottom floors by themselves and peek out from their windows but hardly ever open their doors. Their parking slots end up getting used by other tenants, and no one asks them if it is okay. Las Palmas has a large laundry room, tenants standing around its entrance all the time until it closes at eight. A lot of the older kids hang out on the stairways, well past being bored. There is also a playground with hard-packed sand and a merry-go-round that I can hear the younger kids turn with a loud scrape. That's usually in the early morning, the only time the younger kids are allowed to play there.

I'm at Las Palmas because I got released on a county work-furlough program and this is my housing. After all my talk and my dreaming about leaving Gold Street, about leaving my town, this is where I came back in the end. The job at the paper mill is janitorial and it's only part-time, but I don't say anything about it to anyone. Just saying you work at the paper mill is enough to make people think you've got a good job. Besides, if I don't show up for work, I lose the apartment and the furlough is canceled.

And I know people look at me with some envy because I live at Las Palmas—they know all about this place and why people live here.

I'm lucky: I spent only a year in jail at Avenal, for forgery, paychecks I faked a long time ago. The police were searching for something to charge me with when I got caught in Las Vegas, and all they came up with were those bad checks. I was in Las Vegas, heading east, as far away as I could get from the gas station that I helped rob with this guy I used to know, Kyle, the only white boy on Gold Street. To this day, I don't know what happened to Kyle. He had taken off without me from the motel in Las Vegas, as if he had dreamed something in the middle of the night. I woke up that morning in the motel room, a hard, sharp bang on the door, and then a rattle of keys. It wasn't like on television, with a burst of police shouldering open a room. It was more calm, the motel attendant pointing into the room as if he had known about me and Kyle all along, two police officers and only one gun pulled and quickly holstered.

I can't explain why I hung out with Kyle to begin with, only that he had a hardness in him that came from being picked on when we were all younger, eight or nine years old. By middle school, he'd become a bully and something like a protector for a lot of us on Gold Street, mainly because of his horrible temper: he once picked up his desk and threw it at our social studies teacher and got expelled for a week. When all of us in the neighborhood reached high school, Kyle somehow got a car, a real piece-of-junk Mercury. But in our neighborhood, a piece of junk still cost money, and we never knew how Kyle got the cash—his mother was as poor as everybody else's. We pooled money for gas, and that car got us out of the neighborhood, into Orosi and Cutler, where we'd fling bottles at kids on bikes and steal beer from mini-marts to get drunk in the orchards. Somewhere along the line, after Kyle dropped out of school and was getting into serious problems with the police, it became just me and him: the other guys in the neighborhood stopped hanging around with us. A lot of them had fathers who came over to Kyle's house and yelled at his mother, or beat their own kids and threatened to kick them out of the house. My mother never seemed to know anything about what I was up to, how I broke into one of the elementary schools in Orosi and stole a computer. She believed me when I said I bought it from the high school because it was old and they were replacing all the machines. She didn't know how I picked on some of the junior high kids in Reedley and stole their money, five or ten bucks really, but enough for a case of beer at the mini-mart way out by Minkler, where they didn't care who bought.

Kyle had made no secret about wanting to leave town, but he didn't seem to grasp how hard it was going to be for someone who had dropped out of school. One of the last times we hung out with some of the guys in the neighborhood, out getting drunk in the orchards, he said, "I'm moving down to Los Angeles this summer—do construction like my dad." Someone had laughed at him in the dark. "How you going to do that, Kyle? You're stupid as fuck." And everybody except Kyle had laughed in the dark. Kyle turned quiet. You couldn't hear anything but the swig of the beer in the bottles, no one saying anything. When we left, Kyle floored it back to town, zipping past the stop signs, and the guys in the backseat shouted for him to slow down. At the high school, he stopped and said, "Get out." All of us got out of the car quick, even me, and I felt bad because I had never laughed at Kyle. I had never made fun of him, and I thought he knew that. It was almost a relief when he called me back in and I closed the door. "They're a bunch of pussies," he said, driving down the street, and I felt glad that he wasn't angry with me.

But what he did next should have told me everything. Without saying a word, he drove calmly into the center of town. On Tulare Street, he cut into one of the alleys, turning off the headlights and pulling up as close as he could to the darkness behind one of the trash bins. "Move your leg," he said, reaching for the glove compartment, and when he popped it open, I saw the steel black of a gun. I froze at its heaviness, how cold it looked, a coldness I could feel without even having to touch it. I'd never seen a gun in my life, but it was like running across a snake out in the vineyards, the way you move away from it immediately. He pulled it out, opened the car door, and walked over to the back entrance of the men's clothing store, where he had a job in the stockroom. Kyle calmly shot at the doorknob, and I grabbed at the armrest at how loud it was, the alley ringing its echo. But he was so calm. It was only after he had wrestled the door open that he began to hurry, racing inside and coming back with an armload of jeans, packages of underwear.

"Start the car — don't turn on the lights," he told me, running back inside. When he came back with another armload of clothes and got in the car, I was panicked, listening for the sirens, but there were none. "Drive," he said. "You're keeping all this stuff at your house." Beneath the second pile of clothes, he unzipped a black banker's bag and counted out the cash.

I should have known then that he was after an easy answer, but that was my problem back then. I never thought about consequences. I never thought about what can happen down the road. I never believed that one thing really does lead to another. I couldn't see things coming.

THOUGH IT WAS JUNE and over a hundred degrees, I helped Treviño in the early evening, after my shift at the mill. I would come over after six when his backyard was in shadow, late enough for Treviño to think that I had worked a long day but still had energy and time for him, that the extra money was important for somebody like me, somebody trying to change and get ahead. Treviño, though, was turning out to be cheap and guarded, expecting a lot from the transformation of the yard. I would lug pipes—iron, plastic, and ceramic—out to the front lawn. Treviño followed me out there, then sent me back alone while he went off to a neighbor's. If things were going to sell, he didn't want to let me in on how much he was actually getting.

On days when I had cleared a good patch and Treviño had hobbled out to the front yard, I spent the time with a trowel on my hands and knees and broke up the hard dirt, watering it down. At first, it was all a mess—the loose soil gathered muddy and quick, and the dirt drank the water far, far down, but I just let the hose trickle out for a little while. Before long, everything started to give way: the weeds, broken beer bottles wedged deep and jagged, beetles scurrying for cover. It was on those days that Treviño lightened up into a warmer kind of man, staring at the rich dark of the earth, and I knew he was remembering as he smoked his cigarettes and coughed.

I had done a particularly long stretch of the yard, from one end of the fence to the other, taking my time all through the evening, and I knew that the sun was edging as close to the horizon as it could before it went dark. Treviño had sold an old toilet, not a crack in the porcelain, that I had muscled over to the front lawn, along with some tire rims that used to be on his Cadillac. He had started up the car and taken off without telling me when he was returning, so I had continued with the work, even watering over the patches I had excavated days earlier, the yard slowly giving itself over to me.

Later the Cadillac chugged into the little driveway on the side of the house; the engine idled a bit, as if Treviño were listening to the car as he would a heartbeat, and then there was silence. Kids in the street were still shouting, but they were being called home because darkness was falling. I walked out to the little driveway, where I found Treviño slowly easing himself out of the car with such care I thought he was in pain. "Oye," he called out to me before I got there to help him. "Take the keys and open the trunk."

Back there was a case of beer, a big bag of charcoal, and paper grocery bags cool to the touch. I peeked inside and saw the packages of beef, the onions, the tomatoes still wet from the produce section. "Bring them out back," I heard Treviño say, and I brought the charcoal over my shoulder first.

His house: the back porch had a wooden door with a screen so rusted I could smell a faint powdery puff come from its wire lacing when I closed it behind me. Treviño reached for a tiny grill he had near the door and wheeled it out to the lawn. "Eat with me," he said. "Chop up that meat in the kitchen." And so it was that I finally stepped into his house and saw how cramped it actually was. The linoleum worn down to black patches near the sink and the stove; the refrigerator so tiny it only reached my chest; the heavy gas stove crouching in the corner; the electric wiring looping cheap and dangerous, as in all the houses of the neighborhood; the sink and the baseboards tilting a little where the house must have been giving way on its foundation; on the table, a half loaf of bread with its wrapper tucked under, and plums still coated with the gray film of the field; a smell in the air like the creak of the boards, like mildew, like dust settled deep in the cracks, like kitchen grease. I could hear the whirr of the swamp cooler in the living room, and a waft of air came from its dark space, but the kitchen held everything in a thick heat.

Treviño didn't turn on the kitchen light, but enough illumination came through the window for me to see what I was doing. It reminded me of my mother, back when I was younger, how dark she kept the house when the sun went down, trying to save every dime she could. I chopped the meat and the tomatoes and the avocados and the onions and brought them out in separate bowls to find Treviño with the coals already glowing in the little grill, and a beer in his hand for me.

"So how did you get a place over there?" Treviño asked me when the first pieces of meat came off the grill and he could take a bite while waiting for an answer.

"Las Palmas?"

"You live with somebody there?"

"No," I said, taking my own bite and hoping that would be enough.

Treviño spoke right through his food. "So how did you get the place by yourself? You have a primo working for you in the county?" He lit a cigarette from the grill, then took a last drink from his beer. "Always helps to have a cousin doing favors, right?" When he put the can down, I could hear the aluminum hit empty against the dirt. The yard had gone quiet, as had the houses on the entire street. I felt he was testing me. He reached for another beer in the ice chest.

I chewed loudly, as if that were slowing my answer; it was dark enough by then that I didn't worry too much about Treviño studying my face, but I felt trapped by his question. I knew I had to come clean. "I spent some time in Avenal. I wrote some bad checks. They lock you up for anything these days."

"Is that right?" Treviño asked me, sipping his beer. In the dark, I couldn't see his eyes, how he looked at me, but the way he responded, the deliberate, drawn-out question, worried me. "Is that right?" he asked again.

"Couple months," I lied, taking another bite, watching the grill. "Yeah." I had been hungry from all the work I had done that evening, but now I couldn't enjoy the food.

Treviño flipped some of the meat and then remained bent down as if he could study it by the meager light of the coals. "You know, I told my daughters about you. About you coming to help out. They told me you killed somebody."

I let out a half laugh, a snort of disbelief, and shook my head. "No, nothing like that. Where did they hear that?"

"You know women," Treviño said, handing me another taco, then tapping the ice chest, encouraging me. "Mentiras. They love to tell lies. Bunch of metiches."

The longer I stayed quiet, the more I played into how smart the old man really was. He was waiting for me to offer up some kind of story about the forgery, something he could match against what his daughters had told him, a counterpoint. Patient, Treviño kept chewing, and I weighed my options: a lie or a bigger lie.

"I used to hang out with a kid," I said, knowing it was wrong to admit it. "I bet I know who they're talking about."

"The white boy in the neighborhood," Treviño said gruffly. "His mama still lives on the street, you know."

"I heard he shot somebody. A robbery. That kid was always trouble."

"He's long gone. Probably in Mexico," Treviño said, and then he laughed, but I couldn't tell if he was joking. Even if it was a joke, just the mere mention of Kyle brought back the possibility that someone would uncover the truth, that the door to my apartment would open slowly one morning like the one at the motel over in Las Vegas, and the police would be there, saying they had caught Kyle, or that they had found the car and my fingerprints all over it, or some such evidence that would put me behind bars for a long time. But that had been four years ago, and Kyle was gone and the car was gone and nobody had ever come forward with an accusation, except in my sleep, and then I'd open my eyes and realize I was still safe.

Treviño was having another beer, and he fished out another one for me. I wasn't finished with the one I had, but I took it. The food sat heavy in my stomach and I wanted to go back to my apartment, but Treviño was in the mood to talk, to sit in the yard watching the dark settle in for the short summer night, just like my mother used to, except my mother would just sit out there quiet.

"I don't know how my daughter knows about you. The youngest one, I mean. The one who keeps asking about you. She's almost thirty years old, so she couldn't have gone to school with you."

"People talk, I guess. Even if they get it wrong."

"So she got it wrong."

I could hear his voice settle at the end — that it wasn't a question, but an invitation to tell about the forgery. So I drank more beer, wanting my head to wrap around the buzz and loosen me. "That kid — Kyle — he had stolen this computer that had this program on it that made documents. So we made up some checks that looked like the paychecks he got from this store he used to work at. Went around to Parlier and Fowler, where the Mexicans cash their checks and, you know . . ."

"That doesn't sound easy."

I searched the darkness for an answer. "I had fake ID cards. And the checks were two hundred dollars here, two hundred there. You know, like I worked for a week at the store. I just wasn't thinking, you know? It wasn't like I could do it again and again or anything, so I paid more in the end for a really dumb mistake."

"Avenal? You spent just a few months there, you said? Doesn't sound so bad."

"I got a record now," I answered, and now it felt like the truth. "It's hard to find work as it is, especially when people think you're a thief."

"Once a thief, always a thief, no?" Treviño huffed. He shifted the coals in the grill, which looked to have died down, and they glowed bright orange again, sparking some and jumping out of the grill's base. "Señor Equis. You don't even know who you are." There was more meat in the bowl, and Treviño laid it on the grill.

"People change," I said. "I changed. I wouldn't steal from you."

"Good," Treviño said. "Because I don't have any money." He laughed and opened another beer.

WHERE WE GREW UP, Kyle and me, you travel along Avenue 416 for fifteen miles over to Selma, straight west, to get to

Highway 99, and just before you get to the on-ramp there's a gas station with a towering lighted sign. I've driven there a million times, all those years I've lived here in the Valley, and it's hard to forget the station light's fluorescent gleam, the hard edge it gives to the grape vineyards all around. Months and months after he robbed the men's clothing store, we didn't hang out; the news about the robbery was all over the front page of the paper, but nothing ever happening to Kyle. All the stuff was at my house, but no one ever came knocking. When the news got old, we started drinking out in the orchards again, and that night, I thought the plan was to go out over to Caruthers and maybe smoke some pot. At the gas station, I sat in the car waiting while Kyle went in there, his baseball cap lowered. I didn't know if he was going to steal the beer or just pay for it, but then I saw him walk up to the counter with a case of beer and pull that gun on the clerk, a Mexican kid, so young, his hands straight up and confused. When had Kyle hidden the gun? How had it happened, this kid lowering one hand to open the register, Kyle in his mad frenzy to yank out as much money as he could? My heart raced, hearing the slow rumble of an approaching diesel truck, just off a long haul on 99. I could see the diesel truck approaching with its barrel of a trailer like a shiny silver bullet—it was easy to think that, hearing what I heard, my head jerking back to the station in horror, in disbelief, and Kyle racing back to the car, yelling, "Go, go, go!" He lugged the beer like a treasure chest, the plastic bag of money in his other hand. I did not see the Mexican kid go down, but I heard what had collapsed him. And I knew even then that all of Kyle's want for change and escape and excitement was impossible to reach. I knew even before Kyle counted the money that there wasn't enough in the bag.

We were eighteen and we were sloppy. "Don't go on the highway," he told me, and so we headed back to town. My hands were shaking and so were my knees: I felt I was tapping on the gas pedal because I was shaking so much. "Don't speed," he told me. My eyes were on the rearview mirror. We drove back to his house and I waited for him to go inside. The front door was open to let in the night air, and I could see the shape of his mother sitting in her armchair, watching television, but Kyle only came and went, his mother never making a move. A paper sack of clothes and the plastic bag of money on the floorboard and the gun tucked under the seat. Why Las Vegas seemed like a good idea, I don't remember, but we pulled down Gold Street and out of our neighborhood very slowly. I looked at my house as if I'd never see it again. We took the back roads heading south, through Visalia, Tulare, then the scattering of little towns before Bakersfield, and it was remarkably easy. There was never a cop car; strangely, my panic began to ease. We headed east up into the Tehachapi Mountains on Highway 58 and the darkness, leaving the Valley behind, and even in the night I knew my life had changed without my wanting it to. The fruit trees were gone, the vineyards. In the dark was the dry rustle of the mountains at the burst of fire season. In the dark was the edge of the desert and its frightening jaws, the long road leading to Las Vegas, the headlights, the ominous signs pointing to Edwards Air Force Base, both of us quiet the whole way. The hours were going by, and at home, I knew my mother would never notice. We pretended our silence was caused by the stark awe of the land stretching on all sides, how it wanted to swallow us in Kyle's beat-up Mercury. But that wasn't it. He had done something beyond terrible, and we knew it.

Kyle wanted to stop at a hotel with a hallway, a door that didn't open to the parking lot, but that would have been too expensive, and I knew there was not enough money in the bag. We would have to stop before Las Vegas, on the edge of the city, where the highway still laced through the desert, and the gas stations appeared almost holy in their glow, that's how dark it was.

We found a room at a motel just off the road, maybe ten miles from Las Vegas, but we could tell it was near, a hazy amber glow stretching across the horizon. The woman at the counter gave us a room on the second floor as Kyle had asked, and then, without Kyle asking, she told us the nearest casino was only a mile farther down the road.

I was tired but unable to sleep. Across the road was a diner, and we walked over. Both of us ate huge, cheap plates of omelettes and hash browns, the food making us drowsy. Kyle said this was how it was in Las Vegas, the cheap buffets, and how easy it would be to live there, but I wasn't convinced. It wasn't going to work, and I knew it; still, Kyle flooded me with promises.

"We could wait tables in the casinos, man," he said, his eyes sunken in the sharp lighting of the diner. They looked almost bruised underneath. "Construction. They're building all kinds of stuff in Vegas now. It'll be easy. We'll find work like that."

He snapped his fingers. The waitress had given us decaf, and I sipped at it, staring out the big plate windows at the glow that was Las Vegas. The city appeared to send out heat rising over the dark desert, and I pictured the Strip, all the people there, rowdy, drinks in hand, counting chips, wishing hard, the city never quiet. I tried to picture someplace where Las Vegas would be quiet, where the lights turned out and buildings went dark.

"I needed to get out of there," Kyle said, looking out the window with me. Then, after I didn't respond, he said, "Don't bail on me, man. I'll rat on you." He spoke quietly, the way he had that night in the orchard when everyone laughed at him. I couldn't turn to look him in the eye.

We paid the bill and left the waitress a big tip. Cars slowed to pull off the road and into the diner's parking lot, though it was very late by then. We waited to cross the road, and the wind whipped around. It had been like that since Barstow, when we had pulled into a gas station and I had found myself unable to go into the little store to get sodas. I had just stood there, afraid, with my hands in my pockets and the desert wind racing. Kyle had gone in and bought them instead, paying for the gas in cash, and I stood watching him, the wind so constant that I wondered why sand wasn't picked up and scattered. When Kyle left, he smiled at the clerk.

"Get to sleep," Kyle said when we got back to the room. "You're driving first in the morning," he said, in defeat, because he knew that there was no easy solution. I had been standing at the window, my hands on the curtains, looking out at the glow of Las Vegas and wondering how I had gotten myself into such a mess. When I turned around, Kyle was getting into one of the beds. He had stripped down to his underwear, and I caught a glimpse of him before he went under—he was the skinniest, whitest person I'd ever seen in my life, his chest caved hollow, and I found it incredible to think how somebody like that could have fired a gun.

"Shut the curtains," Kyle said, and I did, but I left them open a crack so I could see outside. I took off my clothes and slipped into the second bed, my eyes still focused on the lights of the horizon, how they kept shining as the hours passed. From the other bed, I could hear Kyle tossing around, but then he finally settled, started snoring.

I stared out to the glint of the horizon and drifted into sleep, refusing to dream of the Mexican kid falling, falling, falling in the gas station way back there. I closed my eyes to him and shut him out, made myself dream of driving into Las Vegas, except it would be nighttime and not morning. It would be the flash of neon bulbs and electric arrows and tourist traffic and people sticking their heads out of car windows to snap pictures of the shimmer. I was dreaming of being like that waitress across the road in the diner. I was dreaming of the motel room being my home for a little while, opening the windows to let in the morning light, then walking across the road for work. I was heavy into dream when I felt the edge of my bed sink some, the covers shifting, and there was Kyle, not saying anything, just getting into the bed. I could feel the warmth of his skin even though he wasn't touching me, and

I was awake again, wondering if I should speak or not. He didn't move for a while, and since I was silent, he must have thought I had gone on dreaming undisturbed. But I had my eyes open the whole time, watching the lights of Las Vegas, and I felt Kyle push himself over, felt him hard against the small of my back. In the same gesture, he wrapped one of his arms over my stomach and started spreading his fingers downward, but I grabbed his hand.

"No, man. I'm not into that," I said, confused. Kyle didn't say anything and I didn't want to turn around to face him, but he stayed in the bed and I kept staring out at the glint of the Las Vegas lights, wanting to drift back to the safety of sleep.

"It's cool, Chris," he said, slapping me on the shoulder, and he rose from the bed. I barely heard him get back into his own. How long he lay there awake, I don't know. At least as long as me. The hours kept ticking by, and I was too bewildered by the turn my life had taken, by the way none of this made sense, how I hadn't had the courage to ask Kyle what he had been thinking all along. But somehow I did get to sleep, and I never heard Kyle get up in the early morning, never heard him start the car that allowed him to get away. Just the knock at the door, then the rattle of the keys, my eyes opening to the harsh stream of desert light coming through the slit in the curtains, and Las Vegas nowhere to be seen on the horizon.

NOW IT WAS LATE and Treviño was drunk, no room to put down an empty can, his lawn chair surrounded by the discards, the half slices of squeezed lime. The grill still glowed a slight orange: Treviño had put on yet more meat, more tortillas. With his belly full, he had stopped speaking, almost abruptly, and then broke the backyard's silence with a deep, rumbling snore.

"Get up," I told him. "Levántese." I shook Treviño's arm. "Levántate," I said, forgetting my manners. I could feel the give of his flesh, his head cocked back and mouth open as if his body were ready to give up his soul, right then and there, the devil waiting by the glare of the grill's coals. I stared at Treviño for a moment, contemplating the struggle. I didn't know the layout of the rest of the house: the bedroom, the bed itself, the light switch or lamp. Part of me wondered, for a moment, if the old man had to take pills before he went to sleep, and then came a wave of what I now know is the edge of maturity, of growing older. Here was worry, like my mother's, over something as simple as drinking too much.

"Levántese," I told Treviño, shaking him a little harder, and he finally opened his eyes. "Can you stand up?"

He made the motion and I lifted him, my hands around his torso and his hands on my shoulders for balance. My own legs swayed from the beer, but I steadied myself. Treviño said nothing, just gently shuffled his way to the back porch, and I stretched as much as I could, extending an arm to hold the door open into the dark house, my other arm steadying him. Treviño never reached for a light, and I didn't know where to put my hands; suddenly the old man was guiding me, the light from the street coming in through the windows, a weak amber. I bumped into the hard edge of a table in his living room. The carpet, I could tell just by stepping, was thin and cheap, and it gathered in small bumps where it was beginning to lift. We walked down a narrow hallway, the mildewed air of the swamp cooler not able to reach all the way down there, our feet echoing now against a wood floor, and then the old man turned into his bedroom, the smell of talcum powder in the air. It was hot in the room, and I brushed my hand against the wall, searching for a light switch, but found nothing.

Treviño sat wearily on the bed, sighing heavily; then he extended himself without taking off his shoes, his feet still nearly on the floor. His snoring returned and I stood there in the dark, wondering if I should shake him awake again, ask him if he needed anything. Treviño sank further into sleep, deep in dream, his breathing intense. I leaned over and pushed his legs up onto the bed. I untied the old man's shoes and slipped them off his feet, placing them out of reach of the bed's edge so he wouldn't trip over them if he got up to piss in the middle of the night.

Because I was in the dark and because the old man was drunk; because it was late and no one in the neighborhood would be wondering about Treviño's dark house; because my curiosity got the better of me; and because I was drunk, too, having polished off some of the beer with Treviño, I reached into the pocket of his pants and slid the wallet out carefully, like in the movies, waiting for the old man to suddenly grab my hands and send the bedroom into a flood of accusing light. And just like in the movies, the wait was tremendous and agonizing, as if the wallet were really a long, unending ribbon. But I kept sliding it out as gently as I could, and finally it loosened into my hands, fat and still warm from being so close to Treviño.

By the weak amber light coming through the bedroom window, I tried to count the bills, but I could not see clearly. I felt them, though, bills and bills and bills, a whole sheaf of them stuffed into the fold of the wallet. They could have been ones and fives, for all I knew: I had no idea what Treviño had actually sold. Nor did I know if this was money from other sales, money he had been carrying around. I ran my fingers through it, the envy coming through my hands, the want, and the knowledge, too, of how impossible it was to put that desire behind me. It would never be enough and it wasn't worth it, the old man waking up in the morning and seeing the wallet empty. If only, years back, Kyle had known the same thing before he drilled into himself the idea of stealing his way out of his life — how ludicrous it was to think it would work, how shameless. But the wanting — I kept my fingers on the bills, just a little bit, and then couldn't help myself. I took out two bills and stuffed them in my pocket. At most it was forty dollars. I put the wallet down, turned to the darkness of the house to leave through the back door, but it still did not feel like enough. Treviño snored loudly and made no move. So I grabbed the wallet again and lifted two more bills.

I moved back through the hallway and the smell of his house, my hands in front of me, my feet heavy and afraid of cracking against something hard. I could feel the air from the swamp cooler, smell its moldy scent, and it reminded me of the desert outside Las Vegas and the unrelenting wind, the darkness surrounding us, threatening to swallow us up. Nothing back then except our car lights in a little patch ahead of us, and here I was again, in darkness but with no light ahead of me, the hallway impossibly long. But when I hit the living room and could see the light barely coming through the kitchen and the back porch, I moved faster, rushing to get out, and the moment I touched the screen door I started running back to Las Palmas. I tripped over one of the lawn chairs, falling down, scattering beer cans. Somewhere a dog started barking, and in a panic I ran faster, past the house, past the Cadillac, past the empty playground, the parking lot with no cars arriving or departing. I calmed down, climbed the stairs to my apartment as quietly as I could. I reached for my keys and let myself in, shutting the door and stopping right there. I couldn't turn on the light, just stood there, breathing hard, panicked. I fished in my pockets for the money, and I could feel the bills in there, warm already from my thighs, but I couldn't look at them.

I was drunk. I went to bed with my clothes on, the room tilting, something that hadn't happened in years.

I HAD SLEPT THROUGH IT. Sometime in the middle of the night, Kyle had gathered his things and left without me. A floor creak, the rustle of a bag, keys, a door click, even the faint turn of the car's engine outside. My mother had always peeked out from behind the curtains every chance she got. But me, nothing. I slept through everything.

Sometimes, in my first days at Avenal, I thought everything I had seen in the movies about prison was fated to bring me down: the territorial gangs, the drugs, the threats. I couldn't sleep at night because I thought I'd be vulnerable to anything. But I wasn't in prison. I was in a correctional facility, and the people there were just waiting out bad mistakes. Still, in those first days at Avenal, sometimes I dreamed I was sleeping in the motel outside of Las Vegas, my mattress caving a little from Kyle behind me, and in the dream I opened my eyes when I felt the hard, cold ring of the gun barrel at the side of my head, and I would open my eyes for real and I was in Avenal.

I have dreamed that dream more often than I have the one about the Mexican kid at the gas station. It has been surprisingly easy to not think about him, to forget about him. I don't even see his face anymore when I remember. I see mine. I see Kyle in the gas station, and I see my hands raised to ward him off. I see myself falling. I'm in the car, too, waiting to drive Kyle away, but the other me is in that gas station, hands raised, falling and falling.

THE LOUD PANIC OUTSIDE of my own apartment, the neighbors scurrying, doors opening all over Las Palmas, the blare of a fire truck. I opened my eyes and saw, from my window, an orange glow, and I jumped from the bed. Flames shot as high as my second-floor window over at Treviño's house, and the neighbors on the other side of him sprayed futilely with a garden hose. A group of men in nothing but underwear were pushing Treviño's Cadillac into the safety of the open street. Neighbors stood out of the way of the firemen, who were now hosing furiously, but it was an old house and it burned ferociously. A weak spray of water splashed on my window, and I realized it was coming from the side of Las Palmas. Someone was down there, trying to protect our roof from the stray embers. The fire illuminated the street, and I could see people either waving their arms to give directions or folding them across themselves, watching in disbelief.

I didn't move to go and join them. I didn't go down to find out from rumor if Treviño had been rescued. More sirens blared; another fire truck came, and there was a flash of light from someone taking pictures. The smell of the smoke seeped faintly into my room, even though the window was closed. I stood watching, suddenly sober, and I had the strange feeling of watching a sunrise, a sunset, the inevitable taking its time. The knock would come on the door, I thought for a moment, the cops again. But I knew it wouldn't happen. After everything that had happened to me, I was beginning to believe I was lucky. I hadn't paid as much as I should have for my mistakes, but I had paid enough.

I stood at my window, as the neighbors did, watching the fire go out. The house crumbled at the front end, the roof collapsing in showers of embers and sparks. Even from my bedroom, I thought I could hear the neighbors murmur in that finality, that sadness. Tomorrow there would be a lot of sorrow in the neighborhood, a lot of people with faces sagging from a lack of sleep, and mine would be one of them. But I would not go down and find out for myself what had happened. Someone would call Treviño's daughters. The thick smoke, visible even in the night sky, rose and rose.

Eventually the firemen extinguished the flames, and the neighbors lingered while they continued to water down the ruins. Tomorrow they would come to see the remains for themselves. Tomorrow they would wake to see the cords of yellow tape fencing off the gap of land. The Cadillac would be driven away by one of the daughters. The mourning would begin, and the neighborhood kids would be sternly warned not to poke around in the destruction.

Sleep did not come. I stood at the window until I had to piss away more beer, but I walked right back and watched, even after the firemen left and the neighbors returned home, the ashes dark and quiet. I stood watching for hours, dipping my hands into my pockets and feeling the bills, but not wanting to look at them. The morning light came early, since it was summer, and I witnessed the sky turn pink and light purple over what used to be Treviño's house. I kept feeling the bills, and when the morning light arrived in all its clarity, I lay down on my bed and forced myself to sleep.

THE COMEUPPANCE OF LUPE RIVERA

KNOW IT'S HARD to believe, in this day and age, but her name really was Guadalupe. Hard to believe because she was a woman in her late twenties, born right here in the heart of California, with parents who spoke good English. What kind of name is Guadalupe when, these days, it's Terry and Nicole and Kristen? I know some of those girls from the neighborhood who married farmers' sons and dropped their last names. So now they're Terry Westmoreland and Nicole Sargavakian and Kristen Young, but still brown as me and Guadalupe Rivera, my neighbor across the street, who doesn't live there anymore. Lupe

Rivera. I know some wouldn't care to hear about a woman with a name like that, and I would have to set you up somehow different if this were about Terry Westmoreland. Somewhere along the line I would have to tell you that Terry was Mexican. But with a name like Lupe, you already know. And, for the record, it's Lu-peh, not Loopy, not a butterfly swirling around in the front yard. I've heard Lupe correct people all the time, very tartly. "It's Lu-*peh*. You speak Spanish," she'd say to the girl at the ballpark concession stand. "Lu-*peh*," she'd say one more time, collecting her change, and then, as she left, she'd mutter under her breath, "Bitch."

With an attitude like that, it's no wonder that not many people in town felt bad about what happened to Lupe. There was a lot to be jealous of, if you wanted to be. When you're smart like Lupe, you can have a job like union arbiter for the city employees, with your own office and a car to drive around in, even if it is a government one, a beige Dodge Aries. I asked my cousin Cecilia what that job required, and Cecilia told me only that Lupe was perfect for it. "You have to have a big mouth but be a good listener, too," she said. "And a lot of the time you have to tell people what they don't want to hear."

Because of that job, Lupe had a little house on the corner of Gold Street, which was all her own because her parents had moved back to Texas. It says a lot about Lupe that she made the side door to the house the front entrance, building a walkway out of brick all the way to the curb, turning on that particular porch light during the dark hours. She liked to say that she lived on Sierra Way and not Gold Street. Not that it matters. Sierra Way is bigger and it has sidewalks and drainage, but it's just as ugly.

You never saw her out on the lawn working to keep it green, but there was always her latest man tending to it, always someone different. When Tío Nico let me stay here a few months ago, it wasn't long before I saw Lupe's latest actually putting up a new fence all by himself. This was early in the morning, about seven, when I was getting in my car to go to work at my retail job in Fresno, and there he was getting out of his pickup truck. You start to know things when you live across the street from Lupe. Even though his truck was rusty and the tires rimmed with dirt, I knew who had paid for all that wood sitting in the truckbed. He didn't look like just a contractor; he looked like a Lupe type, stepping out of his truck in a plaid shirt, tight Wrangler jeans, boots. I waved over to him as I drove off, just to show I was friendly to Lupe, and I wondered where Lupe ran into such men in the Valley, like they had stepped right out of the advertisements for tejano music, come to life just for her.

That evening, when I drove down Gold Street, I saw the pickup truck still there and heard the hammering even over the music on the radio. Out on the lawn, Lupe's latest had already put up the posts and leveled and nailed in more than half the fence. He tipped his chin to me as I parked, and I pretended to check out his work, flashing him an okay as I made my way inside Tío's house, but he had lost the plaid shirt and was wearing his cowboy hat. Just then, I saw Nicole Sargavakian turn the corner slowly off Sierra Way. So word was getting around about Lupe's latest:

handsome and willing to work out in the sun just for her, hairy
chest just like Andy Garcia, but better because he was right there
on Gold Street for all to see.

I am ten years younger than Lupe and I have to admit that
I knew her better when I was a little kid, when I was eight and
Lupe was just out of high school and taking classes over at the
community college in Reedley. Me and my cousin Cecilia used
to tag along over to the Tortilla Flats ballpark by the elementary
school, walking with Lupe across the railroad tracks like we were
her younger siblings. She would buy both of us sunflower seeds
or a cherry soda or a snow cone while she kept the stats for the
men's softball game, one pencil behind her ear just in case the
other one broke its lead.

Lupe Rivera was always prepared. I don't know where she
got the money, but we never had to dig into our own pockets
when we were with her. She took us straight to the concession
stand without asking what we wanted, and then suddenly we had
a treat in our hands, balancing it carefully as we made our way
up the wooden planks of the spectator stands. On the field, the
guys idled around in their uniforms, some of them tipping their
chins and waving to Lupe. I don't know about my cousin Cecilia,
but I never knew what I wanted to watch more — the guys who
waved over to Lupe or Lupe's fingers on the pencil once the game
started, her hand making Xs and check marks and tabulations that
said everything about how fortunate she was, how lucky she was
to be so beautiful as well as intelligent. I would watch her make
the Xs one after another, and sometimes I would forget about the

guys who would wave to her, their tight arms gripping the bat, like they were hitting just for her. I would look at the *X*s and get a little dreamy, thinking about how smart and beautiful she was, how I could be like her someday if I kept studying. Not like my Tío Nico. Not like him, how he had been sitting one day in the kitchen, making little marks on a piece of paper. When I asked him what he was writing, he sat me on his lap and told me he was remembering. He asked me to spell out the names he was attempting for himself, his friends long dead who had been reduced to the one or two letters he knew by heart. When we were done, he took my paper like a souvenir and folded it away for himself.

I can admit that I was a sad kid, that I was delicado, as Tía Sara would say when she still lived with Tío Nico. I used to think that meant delicate, but later I realized it meant fragile, dainty, weak, and overly sensitive. How it must have confused Lupe at the ballpark, me staring at the *X*s she marked on the paper, my thoughts wandering to the memory of sitting with Tío Nico, and then the tears would start for no reason that Lupe could figure out. I wonder now how she would define *delicado*, how she would give the word her own nuance. She stopped babying me not long after, one evening when the guys on the field waved as usual and I didn't tip my chin at them like I was supposed to. I waved right back, and Lupe looked me straight in the eye and said, "Stop acting like a girl." Her stare narrowed into me like light through a keyhole. After that, she wouldn't let me hold her hand. It made me even sadder as a kid, after she looked at me like that, because she never spoke to me again after she told me who I was.

Despite all of that, I have always wished good things for her. I couldn't dream these things for myself, but I could see Lupe in a bell-shaped dress and getting married at the Baptist church over on K Street, even though she was Catholic. It was the one church in town with grand, wide stairs in front and a towering steeple, the walls built of beautiful dark gray stone and the street shaded with trees that had somehow escaped Dutch elm. That would be the church for someone like Lupe, and we could throw rice without having to stuff it into tiny lace bags first. I suppose it is wrong to assume that only someone beautiful like Lupe could deserve such a scenario, and maybe this is where jealousy comes from: the inability to picture ourselves firmly into the lives we can imagine hardest.

That evening, I saw only what the other people saw. I was outside, having decided to wash my car with the hose in the little light left before sundown, because Lupe's man was still out in the front yard building her fence. His shirt was draped on the last post like a reward, and he was working fast, like he was racing the sunset. I didn't care that Tío Nico kept peeking out the window to disapprove of me. He'd been at his wit's end with me and the way I'd been carrying on. Jilted boyfriends coming by the house and pounding on the door because they'd found out I'd moved here and wasn't living with Tía Sara in Bakersfield anymore. But in Bakersfield, I'd never seen a man like Lupe's. I'd never seen a man be so willing to give himself over like that, to work under the hot sun just to make someone happy. He could have had anyone.

And though I was looking, and Terry Westmoreland kept

driving by, and then Kristen Young and all the other metiches in town, we all knew there was something wrong when that car came up the street. We knew it didn't belong here and we knew that it was looking for Lupe's house because the driver paused on Gold Street and turned gingerly over to Sierra Way — he didn't know how Lupe used her front door. We knew the imminent shadow of trouble. We knew that the squeak of unfamiliar brakes meant the men of the neighborhood had to prepare to intervene. And so people stepped out of their houses while that car idled and then killed its engine. I shut off the water hose, and Tío Nico came outside and stood on the lawn, the neighborhood slowly gathering into itself as it did through every argument, through the rare house fires, through the fistfights, the car bashings from angry ex-wives, the drunkenness of early evening Saturdays, the beating of someone's mother and the shattering windows, the guns flaunted and then desperately coaxed away. The neighborhood inched out of their houses, hands on hips, eyes shaded against sundown, some of the men already easing into the street with order in mind, the younger boys lurking behind them like they knew a rite of passage was theirs for the taking. I watched and remembered that feeling, but I had always stayed on the steps.

A man stepped out of that car and shut the door. Lupe's man had stopped working and walked over to the last post to collect his shirt. If a fight was on the way, Lupe's man wasn't about to provoke it. He buttoned the shirt and listened to the other man ask him, "Hey, Guillermo, how come you left my sister?"

That was all he had to say. I immediately imagined Lupe in her bed with the cool sheets lined against her naked breasts, staring at this Guillermo, finding some way to reward him for his day of hard work. I pictured Guillermo's wedding ring sitting by itself in a tiny bowl on Lupe's nightstand, a pale mark around Guillermo's finger like a mark of shame that he would pay no mind. I imagined that scene, of Lupe receiving him with her arms, knew immediately why the women in town hated Lupe Rivera, and what she meant to their own insecurities, their holds on their marriages as tenuous as spiderwebs. "How come you left my sister?" the man said to Guillermo again, louder, and we all seemed to close in, as if to surround a boxing ring, even me. I was mesmerized by what I had just found out, that Guillermo was a married man, cheating on his wife, and that everyone in this town knew with who. But the men in my neighborhood were watching that man's hands, and then the men swarmed suddenly — had they caught the flash of the knife before the rest of us did? I saw the blood spray and I heard Guillermo choke and collapse, the men shouting orders, everyone in the neighborhood gasping, but I still don't know how the men in my neighborhood sensed it all coming, how they had ever gained that power of knowledge, that readiness to step up to the inevitable.

From inside the house, Lupe rushed screaming to the front yard, but by then it was too late. She wasn't naked, the way I thought she'd be, waiting for this Guillermo inside her house, but had on jeans and a white blouse. The man with the knife knelt in the yard, restrained by the entire neighborhood, and he raised his head to the sky to cry out. Strangely, his cry pierced us more than

Lupe's. It was filled with more woe than Lupe's anguished, "Oh no, oh no, oh no . . ."

When the town newspaper arrived at our doorstep a few days later, it brought clarity to the rumors that were racing like wildfire around town. The front page was plastered with pictures of Gold Street packed with police cars and onlookers. We passed the paper between us, me and Cecilia and Tío Nico, the cheap ink rubbing off on our fingers with each reading. Tío Nico gathered the story as best he could from the pictures, then asked Cecilia to clarify what he might have missed. "That man was getting revenge for his sister," Cecilia answered Tío Nico, raising her voice to him as if he were hard of hearing. "He stabbed him as payback."

Tío Nico seemed to nod in agreement as he studied the newspaper, and then he pointed to the picture of that man kneeling in the front yard, saying sorry to the sky and asking it for forgiveness. Tío Nico seemed to nod in sympathy, and when he put the paper down, I waited a moment before I picked it up. Lupe's house, dark in the cheap ink of the newspaper. Lupe with her face ravaged by tears. The wailing man in the front yard. A photo, taken elsewhere, of the handsome Guillermo. I couldn't take my eyes off it, remembering his hairy chest, raising the paper a little because Tío Nico was staring at me. He had had enough and got up from his chair, snatching the paper from me. "Give me that," he snapped, taking one last look at the front page, his finger pointing to the wailing man. "When grown men cry," he said, "it's usually for themselves."

I thought about that later, when I fished the newspaper out of the garbage can and smoothed its crumpled pages just enough to tear out two pictures: the handsome Guillermo and the one of Lupe "oh no'ing" in her front yard. If the wailing man cried for himself, then who was Lupe crying for? Who did I cry for when I was a little boy, thinking of Tío Nico? Did Tío Nico cry for himself when he sat staring at his page of *X*s and *O*s, trying to remember? Did he cry for himself when Tía Sara left him? I couldn't answer myself, so I stuffed the pictures into my pocket like a terrible secret, but I knew why I needed them. I wanted a reminder that everyone suffers somehow, that we all make mistakes, that bad luck can ruin everything, even for someone beautiful like Lupe. Someone beautiful like her man Guillermo. I wanted something to give me strength to send away those ex-boyfriends who trailed me all the way from where I used to live in Bakersfield with Tía Sara, those boys who made me weak kneed with their pleading, who confused me with their rage and anger. I wanted Lupe as someone to look up to, even after all of this, so that I could set aside the weight of Tía Sara's stare and Tío Nico's disapproval and live my own life, just like she did, no matter that it invited contempt.

"Sergio," Cecilia said to me a few days later, "did you know that guy got stabbed in the neck? Can you believe it? In the neck?" She was helping me wax my car, and we looked across the street. "People are crazy," she said, keeping her eyes for a moment on the half-finished fence. I kept waiting for her to comment on the FOR SALE sign in front of Lupe's house, the windows suddenly without curtains and the bare walls gleaming through. I couldn't say I was surprised, though no one had run Lupe out of town. I don't know how or when the house was emptied or who did it. I was at work when it happened and so was Cecilia. Tío Nico wouldn't say a word about it.

"Do you know where she moved?" I finally asked Cecilia.

"I have no idea," she answered, but she looked over at me knowingly, and the way she did it reminded me of the way Lupe Rivera had looked at me years ago, when I was a little boy, that look of knowing what I was all about.

"I ran into Nicole Garcia," Cecilia said. "She's Nicole Sargavakian now. Remember her?"

"Of course I do."

"She said Lupe moved to Los Angeles."

"How does she know that?" Los Angeles, I knew, was where you could live on a wide boulevard. The men who stepped out of the advertisements for tejano music lived there, waiting to tip their hats to Lupe.

"Word gets around," Cecilia said, "I guess."

I had to look down at the car to keep the knot out of my throat, and then I refused my tears because I didn't want to explain to Cecilia what I was feeling. In looking at the empty house, in knowing that Lupe's whereabouts were already being found out and rumored, I discovered something that made my heart weight down some. I realized suddenly that, during the times my ex-boyfriends had driven up to Tío Nico's house with their unfamiliar cars and their loud banging and their threats, the street had been empty. No one had come to see about the car still shudder-ing outside of Tío Nico's house; no one had come even to check to see if Tío Nico was okay. When I opened the door those times, with the porch light burned out, I saw nothing but the silhouette against the screen coming back to claim me, and the street silent behind.

I let loose the tears, and my cousin Cecilia finally saw. I heard her put down the rag she was using to wax her side of the car, and she walked over to me. "Jesus, Sergio," she said. "You're just too sensitive."

"I just feel so bad for her," I lied, but what did it matter? The pictures I had saved to give me some kind of strength would someday fade, and I swore to myself right then that later that night I'd close my eyes and let myself think of Guillermo the way I wanted to. I had no tears for Lupe Rivera, though I still wanted to be like her, to go wherever she was, to whatever place she had found that would just let her be. I let loose my tears, Cecilia's arm around me, the way I had cried when the ex-boyfriends cried and begged me back. I thought of Lupe in Los Angeles, the way the sun was gentler there, and how you could open a door whenever you wanted. Someone would be standing there and he would be worth the tears, worthy of both praise and longing. Someone in Los Angeles, with its wide boulevards, the long avenues that slithered into the hills with your secrets.

THE GOOD BROTHER

WHEN THE WOMAN FROM next door had come to beat up his mother, Sebastián's mother had not been home. She was at the grocery store, and when Sebastián told this to the woman from next door, whose triplet sons stood behind her with their arms crossed, waiting, the woman cursed at him in Spanish, using the vulgar words that he had never been allowed to use without severe punishment. His little brother, Stevie, had stood next to him; Stevie had heard those words before. The woman from next door had been wearing a pink housedress: sheer, thin-hemmed cloth that showed the dark bra underneath, the broad panties. It had embarrassed him, seeing her like this with her boys behind her, all three of them a year ahead of him in junior high. Sebastián had stood there with the screen door open, letting in the summer flies just as his mother had told him not to do.

How long had he stood there, listening to this woman? Why was it that he could not think of a response to her vulgarities, the things she was saying about his mother, the things she was saying about him, her triplets standing silently behind her? She never stopped cursing, just stood there in her pink housedress and the heat of the early evening, her rubber sandals and heels coated from a day's dust, their dirt yard hard-caked from the drought that spring.

When Sebastián's mother pulled up to the side of the house, carefully steering the car onto the thin rows of gravel set down to guard against winter mud, the woman from next door paused in her yelling and just stared with arms akimbo. The neighbors from across the street had come out, pretending to mind their own business, but this was Gold Street, where everything sounded familiar, even cars. These neighbors had known the sound of his mother's Chevrolet, the brown one that had belonged to their father who had long since gone, and they had recognized how much slower she drove it. Sebastián's mother, that Mrs. Jiménez — such a careful woman.

Sebastián's mother had not been able to ask what was going on before the woman from next door rushed at her and grabbed for her hair. That is how it had begun: His mother's purse had been knocked out of her grip, along with the paper cup of soda that she must have purchased when she'd filled up the car at the gas station. Sebastián had watched it tumble away from his mother's hand, the soda she would always give him sips from, his focus for a slight moment on the cup instead of on the punch landing across his mother's jaw. There had been that simultaneous spilling — the parched yard soaking up the soda, a flash of spittle and maybe blood from his mother's mouth — and then her anger overwhelmed her confusion. Sebastián's mother tussled with the woman from next door, pulled her to the ground, and by then men from the neighborhood rushed over to stop them. The men had appeared hesitant, not sure how to pull the women away from each other without touching their breasts, their thighs. It must have been the same shame Sebastián had felt when the woman from next door had first come over, how despite the vulgarities she had yelled at him, he could not keep his eyes away from the dark outlines of her bra and panties.

The police had arrived, their car sudden and speedy on the street, kicking up dust. There had been no sidewalks in their neighborhood then, no curbs next to which the police could conveniently park, and so they had lurched the patrol car onto the dirt yard and left the engine running. The men who had separated the women put up their hands as if to say, *All yours* — they didn't want any trouble. The officers had no difficulty handling the women, pulling both of them back, and one of the officers had spoken Spanish to them. "Cálmense, cálmense," he had urged.

Who had translated while Sebastián remained motionless at

the screen door, still letting in the flies? The triplets gave their version to the police officers, but when one of the neighborhood men overheard them trying to portray their mother as the victim in the ordeal, the man verified that it was that woman and her kids who had started everything—they had all seen Sebastián's mother drive up to her own house. She still had her groceries in the trunk of the car; they pointed at the soda cup in the dust, her purse knocked over, its contents somehow still inside.

The police officers put the woman from next door in handcuffs. They made her a dark silhouette in the rear seat of the patrol car, the neighbors looking on in satisfaction. Sebastián had heard his mother call him forward, and for the first time, he and Stevie stepped onto their dirt yard and saw where the scuffling had drawn up the fresh, dark earth in patches. His mother had ordered them to bring in the groceries, had handed him the responsibility of her keys. She pointed to the car, told them to hurry and get the cold things first. Sebastián brought in the gallon of milk and two packages of chicken legs, Stevie the iceberg lettuce and tomatoes, his mother preoccupied with the business of the officers. Once inside the house, he couldn't hear what was going on, so he set the items on the table instead of immediately putting them away and rushed back outside.

This was years ago, when he was twelve and Stevie just a kid, and yet Sebastián still remembers it. He had gone back outside, and there was his mother shaking her head at the officers and pointing at the triplets. She had been pleading with the officers, and Sebastián had been too far away for too long, just that brief moment, to understand what had happened. His mother had pointed at the woman next door because the woman next door was not just a woman next door — she was a mother, and there was no one to take care of those three boys, no matter if they were already in eighth grade. They were still boys, still children in the eyes of the law, no matter what they had done to her son to cause such disruption. This was years ago — so many years ago, back when their groceries held a carton of RC cola in tall bottles, and the store took back the empties; back when his mother drove them to the Fulton in Fresno, where the city had paved over a road to make a pedestrian mall; back when the Canada Shoe Store was still open, where his mother went only to look but once in a while treated herself to a blue and white box; back when the Woolworth's in Fresno had an escalator, where children were scolded all afternoon for running up and down its metal steps; back when the new town pharmacy sold ice cream cones for ten cents a scoop on Fridays only; back when the new town pharmacy was still new, still open.

So many years ago, yes, and yet how Sebastián would remember those things so sharply and not this, how his mother had changed such a situation.

"Sebastián," she had called out to him. "Come here," she instructed him, and he remembers going to her, wishing he could stay out of the way, distant from the police officers and their polished boots in the dust. "I need you to tell them what happened," she had said. "Tell these officers why you boys were fighting."

• • •

THE WOMAN NEXT DOOR is named Ana Martínez and her triplet sons are Carlos, Cristian, and Claudio. The father fled long ago to Mexico, leaving Ana to care for the triplets from very early on; his name is Ignacio Martínez, and Ana has kept his name and has passed it on to her three sons. The house she has raised them in is in her name and her name only. She has paid for it with hard seasonal jobs in Parlier, Sanger, and Orange Cove and even as far west as Lemoore. Ana has worked in a poultry factory (where she accidentally chopped off her left thumb tip); in a fabric assembly line, tending denim; in the hot, open-air canneries sorting summer fruit; in the fields, picking tomatoes on the east end of the Valley, sorting them into the light green plastic baskets only as big as her hand. She has all the old standbys of such jobs tucked away in her bedroom closet, just in case a similar job ever comes around. Up there are the heavy work gloves, the cannery aprons with their periwinkle designs, the yellow plastic hairnets, the knives with the curved hooks for cutting grapes. Ana has successfully cheated welfare for years, lying about some of her income so she can keep feeding the boys, her troubles always three times as weighty as anyone else's. It has been surprisingly easy to get around the system, even with her jumping from seasonal job to seasonal job and her shoddy English. At the high school, the town offered free English classes in the summertime, and Ana had tried attending but quit almost immediately. The class was taught by an older white woman who had promptly sent her students to the community college in Reedley to buy books for the class. When Ana saw the forty-dollar price sticker on the cover, she had stood in the aisle of the community college book-store weighing such a cost and had determined that it was too much money for a class that was allegedly free.

As her boys grew older, Ana sent them out to earn their keep, and she has thus raised her sons to know the value of money and of helping each other out. Sometimes she is bewildered by their lack of good sense. Had they not witnessed how hard she had worked for them? Why was generosity with money the only les-son they had learned? There are only two of them now: one died when he was seventeen. Carlos had been driving a motorcycle with a neighborhood boy, broadsided at a rural intersection. Both boys had been killed: hers instantly, the other at his own home days later. Of the two sons that are left, Ana sometimes feels she has only one: Cristian is serving time in a correctional facility down south in Avenal for holding up a gas station. Thankfully, he did not kill anyone.

So it is: once Claudio married and had children, he and his new wife convinced Ana to rent out the little house. She lives now in her own one-room apartment on the good side of town. Monthly she travels to Gold Street and collects the rent from the Mexican couple who live in her house. They are good people and keep the place clean; they've planted a row of tall rosebushes in her front yard to please her, and what used to be a hard dirt yard is now so green and plush she wants to walk barefoot on it. The old neighborhood has changed. Sidewalks. Street drainage. Curbs. The houses are now owned by people she remembers as children, and they all have jobs and brand-new cars.

There is that boy, too, from next door when her sons were little: he is a man now and full grown, but the little brother she does not see as much. That house has been transformed, too — a fresh coat of paint every few years, grass and shrubbery, a thin driveway of rocks and gravel. Ana knows it is the older son who takes care of things now. For some time, she thought that the mother had died, only because she had not seen her for so long. For months, Ana had carried inside a tremendous sorrow for not having properly thanked that woman or begged her forgiveness for that incident so many years ago. She was too ashamed to appear nosy to ask the couple who rented her house about the woman next door. Then one day, Ana saw her being helped into her son's car. The woman had aged tremendously, and she appeared to have trouble walking. Ana had waved to her, but the woman was bent in concentration, easing herself into the car. She had not noticed Ana, and so Ana got in her own car and drove back to her side of town. She is so ashamed to admit that she does not know that woman's name.

SEBASTIÁN STILL LIVES WITH his mother. He runs many of the errands for the house, does much of the cooking and cleaning, and sits down every month to sort out his mother's bills. His mother broke her hip in a car accident several years ago, and though she healed, he thinks the accident destroyed the resolve and rigid demeanor that he used to know. She seems to have tired of doing so much and now relies on him to drive her to the store or to the shopping centers in Visalia.

Sebastián feels suckered into the position: his little brother moved out of the house right after high school, down to the South Valley, around Avenal. Stevie is training to be a guard at a correctional facility; he claims to work the night shift, which makes it impossible to come visit their mother because he sleeps all day. Sebastián does not know if Stevie is telling the truth, but he envies his way of avoiding any familial responsibility. Of his own life, Sebastián and his mother have an unspoken understanding. Taking care of her, watching their money, there is no way he will be allowed a life of his own. Sebastián has never been in love. He accepts his position in this world much too easily, as if someday (but not now) he will return the glances he receives from the beautiful man in the red Datsun pickup on Tuesdays at the grocery store. Someday his life will begin.

Sebastián, over the years, has watched the goings-on with the new next-door neighbors. He has watched as they transformed the old, weary house into a respectable piece of property, one that could bring a good sum of money, even for this neighborhood. Slowly, Sebastián began working in their own yard to avoid being inside with his mother and the telenovelas. He broke through the dirt yard and brought in new topsoil, layering it with grass and flower beds. The old appliances and the junked Chevrolets that had plagued the backyard were hauled away. There were long weekends of scraping the old paint from the house before he went down to the hardware store and chose a color, not asking his mother for an opinion. He wishes these transformations to their property could change his mother back to what she had been: *Here's self-reliance*, he wants to tell her, *here's self-sufficiency*. Look at their old neighbor in her new car. Listen to the rumors about where she lives now. It is not true that her son is in jail for drug running. That is not where her money comes from. It is not true that the insurance money from one of her dead triplets made the new car possible. *Look at her*, Sebastián wants to say. *You can change.*

Sebastián stands in the backyard, losing himself nightly. This is where it happened. How did something that happened without a word — not one word — transform itself into the fight between their mothers? Who saw them in the backyard of his house, where the debris of Sebastián's father's relentless scouring of yard sales and car auctions left only a legacy of junk? Who looked out a window to see Sebastián there behind a defunct Chevy, kneeling, openmouthed like the hood of that car? Why was it that Sebastián could not recall how many times it had happened, him and one of the triplets, how they had transformed their games into a kind of play he did not fully understand? Why had he trusted that brother, allowed him to put him inside the discarded refrigerator and close the door? Memory cannot restore the answers for him, but the sudden heat and the lack of air, the faint odor of decaying vegetables, always comes back to Sebastián without effort. And yet still he allowed it, over and over, the sealing of the door against the daylight while that brother grinned at him. Because very soon the door would open, and his rescuer would come in a mad rush, pulling him from the confines of this horrible trap and leading him into one of the getaway cars, the one with the hood down so they could see their imaginary road. How had dust entered that car, coated the seats and the steering wheel and the radio knobs, when the windows were always sealed up? *Hide,* he remembers the triplet saying, *they're shooting,* and he would push Sebastián low on the wide bench seat, and this is how it always began. They were too old to be playing like this. They were in junior high.

Look at the backyard now: the lawn chairs and the glass-topped table with a striped umbrella in the middle. Sebastián sits out there in the early evenings, looking west, sipping iced tea and pretending to read the town newspaper. He built that fence from pinewood, leveled it and set the beams in concrete. It will never sag the way the old fences always did. It will never rot in the rain like the one his father built before he went away. The grass back here is the same as the lush green out front. No more tall weeds browning in the summer sun, no more errant trash pushed into the corner of the yard by the wind. A row of sunflowers, small offerings of tomatoes, earth turned over so often it is as dark as his hands. No traces of what the place used to look like, all the old junk hauled away, not a drop of oil, not a speck of rust.

Sometimes, when he is sure his mother is engrossed in the tele-novela, and the evening has come full on, Sebastián gets up from the lawn chair and walks barefoot across the grass. He waters the lawn and the flowers in trickles and pretends to fool with the hose. But he is a lonely young man, and this is why he moves from spot to spot on the lawn, as if looking at the horizon and the sky. He asks himself if he is standing where the old refrigerator used to be, if he is standing on the spot where he once knelt, where he floated below one of the triplets.

Was it the dust and dirt on his clothes that gave it all away? Had someone peeked over to see what they were up to? Why hadn't he driven the car for once, pushed the triplet down to get away from the pursuers, felt the rush of that kind of escape? Which triplet was it—the one in jail, the dead one, or the one who is married? Could it have been more than one? Does cruelty carry over like that, down and through the blood?

It gets darker and darker as evening turns to night. His mother always comes to the back door and reminds him to turn in, and Sebastián always tells her, "Ya voy." He stays there, though, and stops and wonders. He can feel his mother still at the back door, silent. Was this it? Right here? Here?

SEBASTIÁN'S MOTHER WAS BORN Adelina Valdes, and she married Ezequiel Jiménez when she was still very young, and they bought the house she lives in now before the first of her two children had even been born. Next door, Adelina had watched another young couple just like them move in, and one summer she noticed that the woman was becoming larger and larger—she was pregnant, and Adelina envied how their life was going to start. The husband was a handsome man who drove his own work truck. When Adelina sat on the front steps to enjoy the cool of evening, she could hear the husband bang the dust from his boots on his own concrete steps. How polite he was—how well he treated that woman.

Adelina never considered her family poor, even though they struggled. There was always enough to eat — maybe not a full meal, and maybe not extravagantly — but once she was married, she and Ezequiel never went to bed hungry. When she was growing up, her parents had always taught her to accept what she had, to work hard for her own, and never to complain that others had more. Yet there she was, watching that woman becoming larger and larger, and Adelina wanted nothing more than her life: a husband both handsome and thoughtful, a work truck, the thud of boots to knock out field dust and keep her house clean. When the babies arrived early the next spring, the neighbors all came to help her because one woman could not do it alone. They brought the woman food and diapers and toys, whatever they could. Adelina could hear their apologies from her front steps, the neighbors coming during the dinner hour to bring over a dish of food or a small bag of groceries.

Adelina wanted as much grace from the neighbors. She could not bring herself to walk next door and offer her congratulations and her aid. A month later, when it was warm enough to sit outside again during the evenings, Adelina saw the woman emerge from the house with one of the babies. Then the handsome father came out holding two more, and Adelina marveled at the excess — so it had been true. She had watched them load the babies into the truck, the woman getting in first and the husband trying his best to help his wife adjust to holding two in her lap. The third he carried himself, and then he shut the door. Adelina had watched them the whole time, and they had looked over at her, but she had pretended not to notice. She had turned to go back into the house, moving nonchalantly, but she had known those people were better than her in some way. They could have called out to her to get her attention, to say a neighborly hello, but they probably had been raised as she had—never bring attention, never brag.

With Ezequiel, she tried and tried to get pregnant, and when she finally did, Adelina was filled with a dread of expectation. It would not be enough, just one child, and she knew that. All through her pregnancy, she fretted over it, cried during the afternoons when Ezequiel was off working or looking for work. And when the baby arrived, it was Ezequiel who named him. Ezequiel was the one who was proud and excited about the arrival, gave him the name of a cherished uncle from Zacatecas. Adelina had agreed, holding the baby in her arms, knowing it was not enough.

When she came back from her short stay at the hospital, there were no neighbors to greet her. When she wheeled the baby to the town center to buy milk or diapers—an unnecessary trip because she had plenty in the house—none of the neighbors did more than say hello, stopping only briefly to peer at her baby. There was no help coming in the evenings, no bags of groceries. It was not enough, this child.

Adelina had not been raised that way. You love what you have and you do not envy. You love what you are given, and patience brings you more of what you love. She had not been raised to look at another man that way, to memorize him the way she had. She had not been raised to hold her first child in her arms, alone in the daytime while Ezequiel was off working or looking for work, and think such things. Adelina would hold the baby and stare into its eyes and try to love it, but the love would not come.

That guilt is with her again and not forgotten: lately, Adelina has said nothing of the pain, a thick wire of it in her hip that cannot be the old injury from the car accident. Not that pain, the jolt that still comes back to her only as a stiffness that keeps her seated on the living room sofa much longer than she really wants to be. That remnant of pain Adelina can live with. When it keeps her on the living room sofa, there is no way for Sebastián to know that she is in need. Adelina can keep quiet about it. It would do her good, she knows, if she gave voice to her distress, but she already knows that it is too late for that: she has fallen into her son's assumptions that she has reached old age, even though she is still young.

But this new pain: it starts in the same spot, in the damage of the hip, and lodges itself as hot fire in her side. This new pain comes at night, travels farther up her torso every time. As she lies in bed, she can sense the pain pulsing, and in the dark Adelina probes her torso as if she might feel something there. Her body is at work: her blood races, and when the pain grips at her with its particularly fiery hand, Adelina's mouth winces a heavy salt. That taste gathers itself and she rises from her bed at whatever hour to go to the bathroom and spit it out. Adelina has spooned the last remnants of jalapeño slices into a plastic bowl and rinsed out the jar. She keeps this jar under her bed, hidden away from view, and spits into it every night. In the morning, she inspects it, but there is nothing there to signify that fire.

After the car accident, during the recovery, her body seemed to expel everything. Blood came frequently: she would cough it up violently, wrenching her throat, or find it dotting her underwear. Her nose would bleed for no reason as she sat watching television, that heavy metallic taste in the back of her throat that signaled it, and by the time Adelina reached up to feel her nose, there were already drops coming down, spotting the front of her dress.

But this new pain — it brings her nothing. Adelina imagines herself at the doctor's office, and she would not be able to describe what she is feeling without resorting to Spanish. It would make no sense in English. *Como si alguien está adentro . . . no sé . . . así, adentro.* Adelina would want to say that there is another presence inside of her because it only happens at night, and she racks herself trying to figure out who or what would have brought this on so late in life. Adelina has paid all the prices; Adelina has withstood all the fists of daily living. Her husband left her long ago, and today she can still crumble at the finality and certainty of his departure — isn't that punishment enough, the memory that refuses to let her go? She had a car accident, her cautious driving having done her no good as she entered one of the intersections way outside of town. The diesel truck had nailed the passenger side, and the wreckage had torn into her right hip. She'd been so lucky! That she was coming and not going; that the diesel truck was trying to slow down; that she had not been exposed to the open air like the neighbor's son. That poor, poor child. Adelina had known his pain at that moment, had remembered him while she waited for the rescuers to extract her from the tangle of metal and the shards of glass. She had been weeping, not because of the pain, but because of the anticipation and imagination of something worse: her legs could have been hit, dead-on and naked, like that boy. She could have come to know the smell of the hot asphalt, the glass ground into her hands, something more besides the sinister hissing coming from her wrecked car. But instead, except for her hip, she had been miraculously unharmed.

Adelina rises from bed nightly now, restless in that way she remembers her own parents being, hearing them stumble through the small house, tiptoeing across the children strewn asleep on the living room floor. She goes to the bathroom but then finds herself standing at the back door. Did her parents do this, staring out into the backyard at three or four in the morning, fear amplified by the dead quiet of the neighborhood? What was scaring them, keeping them awake?

Sometimes she actually steps out into the backyard, reminding herself that it is a small town and there is nothing to fear at night. The frogs have come out, thanks to Sebastián's persistent watering, and she can hear them plop softly away in fear of her footsteps. Sometimes the rumble of a work truck faintly echoes from several streets away; it is always a heavier sound, the sound of men gathering sleepy in a truckbed to hit the fields on the west side before dawn. Adelina stands barefoot in the grass. She has never had such simple luxuries: if she wants, she can put on shoes;

if she wants, she can sit at the glass patio table her son has purchased. So why is this happening? Who is evil-eyeing this pain into her side when she has done so much to reverse her early faults? Are others free of this distress, or are they better at ignoring it — like her son Stevie in Avenal and his contentedness, or her former husband, Ezequiel, who must live with the self-satisfaction of a man who has fled from what he does not want? Even that woman from next door, her neighbor, despite having lost two sons, still has one to her name, and he is repaying her for everything she has given in her hard life. Adelina knows she has had a hard life. Adelina gave to her, too: she remembers their fight in the yard, the wincing and the pulling, the rings on each of their fists having no purpose anymore but to inflict damage. She saved her children, Adelina thinks, and has yet to receive thanks for it.

Is it Sebastián, then, born the way he was, who is the trial to her expectations? Is he the reason she is now suffering through this? Adelina stands in the grass and looks up at the stars slowly giving way to the coming of dawn. Perhaps he suffers, but there is no way to ask him. She cannot fathom asking her son about his pain, the suffering he must keep burrowed inside — he must have it, no? How can she ask his forgiveness? It would be like asking these stars any kind of question, talking to them when they have no language to respond except to shine back, flash a bit, and then die out.

"YOUR MOTHER WAS A good woman," the brother says, the triplet who is neither dead nor imprisoned, and when he says this to Sebastián and Stevie, it is Stevie who says the thank-you and then, without hesitation, asks, "Which one are you?"

"Claudio," he says. "I'm Claudio."

"I work at Avenal," Stevie tells him and leaves it at that.

"Yeah." Claudio sighs. "Cristian . . . Chris."

The house has been sold and Sebastián has no burden now; Stevie has made all the decisions and does all the talking. Stevie was the one to send a letter via family friends to their father in Mexico, and although their father did not appear at the funeral today, no one had actually expected him to. Stevie had already looked into the legalities of selling the house to help pay for their mother's hospital costs, and with a lawyer's help, he registered papers with the courts declaring their father's default of ownership owing to absence.

Sebastián thanks Stevie, in his heart, for saving him from this. He thanks Stevie, silently, for giving him new life.

Their mother's illness was broadcast to the neighbors via the rush of an ambulance early one evening, five minutes before the start of her telenovela, when she had collapsed on the living room floor and called out Sebastián's name. Sebastián will never forget that, how she called his name with all the volume she could muster. Twice she called it, and he rushed to her from the backyard, dialing emergency, and while he spoke to the woman on the other end of the line, Sebastián half expected to hear his brother's name come from his mother's mouth. He felt guilty about it afterward, when the doctors said it wasn't a heart attack or a stroke or an aneurysm, but a cancer already grown large. His mother was not dying right then and there, but she was close, and he had wished her to declare whom she really needed. A bad wish, a terrible want. She had called his name for help, nothing more or less.

They are standing a bit away from the burial site, watching the dismantling of the tent propped up to give shade to the mourners. Efficiency and respect drive the cemetery workers: the little tractor is somehow quiet as it scoops dirt into the grave. There are no men with shovels, working nobly while family stands to watch, as would have been done in the old days. Only a little tractor, two men folding up the chairs and loading them onto a waiting truck, two more men rolling up small sections of carpet laid down around the grave site. They stand and watch out of finality, Sebastián and Stevie, but Claudio waits with them for a moment.

"Well," Claudio says finally, when his little girl comes running for him, oblivious to their seriousness, "you know the directions to the house."

Such is his grace: if their mother had only known how many of the neighbors from Gold Street had come this morning, it would have surprised her. Sebastián never heard as much come from her mouth, but he knows how she felt disregarded. What would she have said to Claudio's offer to have food in the backyard of his house, to Claudio's mother making the rounds of the Spanish-speaking neighbors, inviting them to come and honor the woman who had lived in that house over there, no need to bring food because she would do much of the cooking? Was it, Sebastián wonders, all done because the woman from next door knew they had no immediate family here? Was it, he wonders, because she knew what it meant to have a father leave, had felt the void that fathers create by severing a broader reach of family? She has been saved, this woman from next door, by the appearance of her first grandchild, the little girl tugging on her father's leg. She has been justified.

"You know your mother was a good woman," Claudio says again. In his dark suit, he is so handsome, Sebastián thinks, and his heart wonders if Claudio is the one from his childhood, the one from the backyard. What would it mean now? What if it is not him?

"She saved my mom," says Claudio, looking back at the cemetery men. "Did she ever tell you that? That day when the cops were going to arrest my mom for that fight? Remember that? We could've been dragged off to children's services. Foster homes, even, because we didn't have anybody here."

The woman from next door is over by the cars lined at the side of the road. She is waiting but does not come over. When she passed through the receiving line, she had said his name, "Sebastián," and then hugged him, and he had been ashamed of what she knew of him. Then even more ashamed as he stood through the service, knowing that at least one person knew the answer to his real secret. She had known his name. All along she has known his name.

"She did her best," Stevie says. "But I gotta tell you, our mom didn't really mention it at all."

"Seriously, man?"

"Seriously."

The little girl is tugging at Claudio's leg more and more, so Claudio picks her up. "She's getting bratty," he says, "so we'd better go. See you guys at the house." And as if he were departing for a long journey, Claudio leans over and hugs Stevie, one-armed but close, slaps him on the back, and even though the little girl is in the way, Sebastián can see Claudio's eyes close as he does this.

It is all the same, those eyes, the sighing and the moans, Sebastián's longing and wishing, his memory always going back to the backyard that does not exist anymore, to a nameless boy whose body was ripening in adolescence, but Sebastián had been too young to understand what he was receiving. There is no way to go back to it. There is no way to go back and uncover the tracks of its anonymity.

"Sebastián," Claudio says, and he reaches over to hug him as he did Stevie. Sebastián closes his eyes, can feel the proximity of Claudio's little girl and her lace dress, the sticky-sweet smell of all children. He takes Claudio's offer of condolence but feels the shape underneath, the solid back, the shoulder. Whether this is the brother or not, the shame of what he is doing so conflicts him that Sebastián begins to cry. At what, he does not know. Like Claudio's mother, he has been released from a kind of imprisonment, and he can begin a new life now. But here he is trapping himself, feeling this man's back and willing memory to rekindle some kind of happiness, if happiness is what he had been feeling way back then.

"It's all right, man," Claudio says, patting him on the back. "You took care of her. She loved you guys, man. It's all right."

THE FAITH HEALER OF OLIVE AVENUE

EACH BOX OF PAPER — regular business paper for copy machines and office printers — weighed 40 pounds, and they had been stacked the way they were supposed to be, eight in each layer, laid not side-to-side, but crosshatched for balance. Each row was 320 pounds, pressing down on the wooden pallets that the company kept using and reusing, through winters of deepening fog that dampened their rigidity, through summers that dried them out again. Each row contained that much pressure, each pallet stacked four rows high, the boxes crosshatched for balance, which meant you alternated the position of the boxes so

that when it came time to unload, the pallet wouldn't tip over—
a danger, especially if the handler was a kid who didn't know what
he was doing. Emilio was twenty-one at the time. Four rows high,
each row 320 pounds. More than half a ton: 1,280 pounds of paper. Simple paper. Cheap paper, too, the kind you could see right
through if you held it up to the light. Usually when the pallets
were shipped, they were wrapped in plastic, around and around,
to hold the boxes in place. Paper was like eggs: the moment a
box was dented, the paper became garbage. Imagine trying to
persuade the insurance men over in the old Guarantee Savings
Building in downtown Fresno to have their secretaries run reports on paper that had a big fold in the corner, a ripple at the top.
And Fresno was just thirty miles away; shipping there was easy.
Still, you had to be careful. Pallets shipped all up and down the
West Coast, mostly to Los Angeles and Seattle and Portland, and
any of the boxes headed to San Francisco were actually bound
for Honolulu. That was a long ways from home, a long ways for
something to go wrong, for a pallet to tip over and break open like
a carton of eggs. That kind of thing cost money, and since plastic
was cheap, it made sense to have the teenagers who did the wrap-
ping just keep circling the pallets. But that was during the regular
day shift, Shift One, when the paper mill hummed along with the
rest of the Valley and the trucks came almost one after another,
and the majority of the workers were women, who needed to be
home with their kids later. Shift Two ran from roughly five in the
evening until one in the morning; in the summer, the crew on that
shift didn't have it so bad, since the paper mill was so far out of

town that in July you could actually still see the blood-line of the sunset on the horizon until almost ten at night. Emilio worked in Shift Three, the skeleton crew who came in at one in the morning to keep the paper mill and its machinery going all night long, cleaning up the warehouse, making it ready for the arrival of the real crew, forklifts darting around like mice to rearrange everything so it was neat like a grocery store when it first opens in the morning, all items in place. Teenagers were not allowed to work at that hour, so if a pallet had to be prepped for shipping, you either called up one of the other guys on the floor or you did it yourself. On that particular shift, Emilio had been out on the loading dock, smoking a cigarette, keeping an eye on his watch. When his fifteen-minute break was nearly over, he had jumped down to the dirt below and scuttled quietly into the adjoining grape vineyard to smoke a joint. Lately, the paper mill had had so much trouble keeping Shift Three fully staffed that management basically turned the other way when the men disappeared into the vineyard to sneak whiskey, a joint, whatever kept them going in those odd hours when the world disappeared completely into sleep. Out in the vineyard, Emilio could smell pot wafting down the rows, hear leaves parting and boots in the dust. Shift Three was nothing but former high school troublemakers, or family of management, all men, mostly single, and generally suspicious of each other. Ask Patricio, the one they had fired just three weeks ago after someone ditched his own joints into Patricio's work shirt, which was hanging in the break room, during a surprise inspection. This was why Emilio, despite having already had more than a few sips of whiskey, hurried with the joint, trying to savor it a little before smothering it into the thick dust of the vineyard, not wanting to be late back to his post. This was why, once back at his post, he hesitated to ask someone to help him wrap the pallet he had to forklift over to the opposite wall for shipping at nine sharp. Stubborn, Emilio tugged a few sheets around alone, a difficult job because the plastic almost adhered to itself, exactly the way it did when his father tried to wrap up the leftovers plate after dinner. Three sheets around, he quickly looked to see if anyone had noticed, and then scrambled onto the forklift, hoping to get the pallet over where it was supposed to be and let the morning crew worry about it. When he raised the pallet, though, the forklift let out a metallic groan and jerked to a halt just when the load was about six feet off the ground. Jiggling the controls did no good. His senses heightened into a mild paranoia about being caught with whiskey on his breath, Emilio gunned the forklift one more time, but to no avail. He jumped down from his seat and leaned a look into the front end of the forklift, seeing almost immediately what the problem was: one of the chains had jackknifed out like a broken bone. Putting his hand forward to touch it, Emilio flinched immediately, recognizing the danger. But just as he let go of his stubbornness and was about to yell down the warehouse aisle for help, the wood of the pallet creaked with a sound that reminded him of an old bridge back in Texas, the sensation of looking down into a cold, racing creek. But Emilio was looking up at the ill-wrapped boxes of paper collapsing, the wooden pallet splintering and suddenly shifting the entire weight of the load. The forklift itself could not handle the distribution, either, and it came crashing down, rolling over on its side, Emilio futilely raising his hands to the massive amount of weight. All of those men who had been in the vineyard had come running and he had heard them screaming, but Emilio couldn't let any sound out of his own mouth. He had felt the blood drain away around his legs with every painful thump of his heart. The cement floor of the warehouse had gone slick with blood — dark red, almost brown, against the gray — and Emilio had turned his head to see work boots leaving faint footprints of it as the men struggled to lift off the boxes of paper, one at a time.

His father lifted him, both hands reaching upward into Emilio's armpits, and struggled — his father was too old for this. He lifted Emilio from the lip of the toilet and slid him into the seat of his wheelchair. Morning's call was done, a little coffee and a cigarette to force the bowels, but the process was taking longer these days. How did it feel, he wanted to ask his father, around his arms? Was he losing too much weight? Lately, Emilio couldn't tell if his father's bony hands or the disappearing muscle tone around his own arms was to blame for the discomfort he felt while being lifted. His father sat on the edge of the tub, exhausted, and Emilio maneuvered his wheelchair closer to the sink so that his father could get up and leave the bathroom, but he would not budge. Twice a day his father had been doing this, for almost a year now, and the complaint had always been present in the way he averted his eyes from Emilio. At first, during the initial months of recovery, when Emilio had no choice but to use a bedpan, he grimaced and closed his eyes whenever his father entered the room to inspect the pan for evidence that Emilio needed attending. *Embarrassment* was not the word; neither was *shame*. Those words were too easy for how Emilio felt when he turned his head away, listening to the baby wipes being pulled from the plastic container, two at a time. It would be easier, the doctor had told him, once a few months had passed and the strength came back into his arms. He would have mobility, dexterity in his fingers. Remembering this, Emilio would flex his fingers as his father finished up, letting out a small laugh that only made Emilio close his eyes. "I did this when you were a baby," his father would say, as if it were of no consequence, but surely he was mortified by the bedpan he had to empty daily. Months later, in late autumn, when Emilio was more mobile, he had discovered that his shoulders could not sustain him as he tried to lift himself from the toilet for the very first time; Emilio had struggled to pull his underwear and pants back on, listening quietly to the television in the living room before finally yelling out to his father for help. For the rest of that day, Emilio had sulked in his room, as if he had many possibilities to weigh, as if the problem before them required only identifying the right relative to ask for help. From the floor of his room, he had grabbed two books, a dictionary and a Bible, and lifted them as if he were back in his high school gym pumping out a shoulder press in preparation for football season. He stared intently at the bare white wall of his room as if it were a mirror at the gym, willing his shoulders to regain themselves. In the mall over in Visalia, when he was a teenager, hadn't he seen some of the older Vietnam vets wheeling around, arms loaded with muscle, one even with a pretty woman stroking his forearm as they looked at jewelry? But he put the books down, defeated, his shoulders pinching with fatigue, what used to be a good pain, good memories of the strain of racing down the edge of the field on Friday nights, hamstrings tight, chest pounding, the feet behind him unable to catch up. Underneath the mattress, because he had counted on his father's generally slovenly nature, Emilio had hidden some of the pills he was supposed to have taken long ago. For days like these, when he knew his mind would not allow him any consolation, he was grateful for them, and he positioned himself on the bed so he could reach them more easily. A pill under his tongue, then swallowed, and then he would watch the ceiling blur away as he slept — would this be his existence? His father's exhaustion on the edge of the tub said otherwise. "Apá," Emilio finally said, "what's wrong?" He looked past his father at the old lead pipe, dragged from the backyard, that his father had bolted into the tub's sidewall to help Emilio gain leverage so he could bathe. He pictured his father trying to think of ways to help him when he had no real way of doing so. How many afternoons had Emilio lain in bed, watching the ceiling blur away, the faint sound of a hammer pounding nails into wood, the back-and-forth of a saw in tired hands? All this time — almost a year now — the ramp had been waiting for him from the front door out to the rest of the world, but Emilio had never used it. Ignoring his father's invitations — his pleadings — to leave the house, Emilio only wheeled into his room and slammed the door. But here was his father now, tired, sitting on the edge of the tub in a bathroom that was ill equipped for Emilio, the house itself too old and small for him to be comfortable, and his father looked like Emilio must have, all those months ago, sitting on the lip of the toilet and wondering how to ask for help. "Apá?" he tried again, hoping almost perversely that something was physically wrong with his father, something to explain the empty pause in his father's life, something to rid them both of the obligation. "No puedo," his father sobbed, choking the tears back the way he used to when he drank, years ago when Emilio was a little boy. "No puedo," his father said again, his words strangled thoroughly with defeat. There was no answer Emilio could give — not after his father's efforts with the tub, with the ramp that Emilio had yet to use, with his almost year-long refusal to exit the house, even to see the doctor. If his own heart could not settle comfortably around his deterioration, what must his father have been thinking all these months, as he sat in the next room? All over town — all over this street, Emilio knew — fathers abandoned their children all the time and fled to Mexico, allowed themselves to be swallowed up by that country. Little children, unable to fend for themselves, four or five of them at a time, the oldest one guarding the door and watching the oven flame for dinner. Somewhere in men like that lay the answer to why love could not override guilt, and maybe the same virus crept in the blood of Emilio's father. Adults were adults, even Emilio, un hombre. As they sat in the silence of the bathroom, his father still crying, Emilio contemplated what he might have to do if he were alone, but the possibility of a stranger lifting him from the toilet instantly stymied him. "Allá en Fresno vive una curandera," his father said suddenly, before Emilio could imagine himself in their kitchen with the linoleum worn down to its black core. So there was his father's solution: a faith healer over in Fresno, a witch woman. When his father said no more, Emilio realized that he had spoken of a faith healer not as a request but as a demand. People his father's age gave utmost respect to the power of the body, no matter how much they damaged it with heavy drinking, with Mexican bread in the morning, with the lard set to frying in a pan for every meal. The body persevered no matter the circumstances, was made to perform the way it did when Emilio played football. They never understood how hard it was to maintain a physique like that, and for every minor muscle tear, every time he had come limping off the field, he knew his father had been scanning the bleachers for the person casting the evil eye. In the awkward, translated dialogues with the doctors after the accident at the mill, Emilio had shuttled back and forth between the doctors' refusal to admit how grave things were and his father's underlying suspicion that black magic was at the root of it all. Emilio would have dismissed the idea, too, had he not remembered seeing what he had seen: the black bile his father had thrown up for weeks when the witch woman cured him of his alcoholism; an egg swept over the body of a cousin in deep fever, then cracked bloody red into a glass of water; the months of calm, just before his parents' divorce, when the curandera ordered his father to strip the bed of the quilt made by his mother-in-law for their anniversary. He believed in these moments as much as he did in the fate that had toppled the boxes of paper to put him where he was: nothing could explain them, but nothing could negate them, either. His father wept as he sat on the edge of the tub, inconsolable. Emilio reached for the faucet, washed his hands clean, arched over to rinse his face, gathering the water in his mouth as if he were gathering this moment, spitting it into the basin, wishing it away. He unbuttoned his shirt down to the navel, cupping a handful of water and bringing it to one armpit, then the other. At Catri's house when they had been dating, this was what he had done in the deep hours of the night, washing himself down while her parents were sleeping, Catri begging him to be quiet, to run the water only a trickle so the pipes wouldn't wake anyone up. He checked his face in the mirror and decided against shaving, the bother of it, and buttoned his shirt again slowly. Still, his father would not look up from his crying. So finally he said, "Let's go, then," and backed out of the bathroom, wheeling himself to the front door, down the narrow hallway where his father had been forced to roll up and put away the long plastic runner that had protected the carpet. At the door, he felt like a cat waiting patiently to be let out for the morning; he could hear his father creak the bathroom floor with his weight as he walked to his own room. Emilio did not know if he had retreated in defeat, the way all of his relatives did when confronting each other, slouching away from an argument only to relive it differently when telling about it later. But before long, his father ambled down the hallway and he eased past Emilio in the chair to open the front door, cowboy hat and car keys in hand. And there outside was the ramp, its wood brand-new and smoothed, sloping gently down to the front yard.

As if the wheelchair were a part of him, his father gripped the handles hard as they exited the house; the ramp sounded like a lakeside dock, planks shifting, the chair's front wheels precariously close to the edge, with no rails to hold them back. They eased down the ramp together, Emilio at his father's mercy as his old hands struggled some to keep the wheelchair from pitching forward. Would the ramp ever feel less steep — was it the unfamiliarity? The ramp's edge came down to the grass of their front yard, and Emilio bore down on the wheels to help his father move him along. At the car's passenger side, his father opened the door and positioned the chair as well as he could, and then the real effort came, a greater effort than Emilio had known all this time — his father had to lift him to his feet to get him into the car. The pain shot through his armpits again as his father lifted, and up he went, helpless and relying completely on his father's strength, floating in the space between the car and the safety of his own chair. Such second nature to get in a car, Emilio thought, how you got in and lowered your head just so, the rarity of actually bumping your head. But now his body tensed up, out of his own control, and every shift of his father's legs for leverage made Emilio anticipate being dropped; but instead his father lowered him bit by bit onto the car seat, and with relief, Emilio pulled the whole dead weight of his legs into the car on his own, and then his father shut the door. They were headed toward the answer to this dependence. Without speaking, his father started the car and backed out into the street. All his life Emilio had lived here. Leaving home had been inevitable, like marrying Catri, just a matter of knowing when the time was right; but here he was, still on Gold Street — and now he always would be — among the houses either crumbling down at the foundation or boasting a fresh coat of paint. He counted the houses on his side of the street as they drove along, skipping the vacant lots, the new apartment complex, Catri's house with no cars out front today. Fifty-nine houses before they reached the stop sign and headed for downtown. One hundred and twenty houses, or thereabouts, each of them with some combination of parents and children or newlyweds, so many people, and after a year probably some Emilio did not know. What change in a year of not leaving the house. Downtown, his father pointed out the new movie theater with its single screen, the renovated stretch of L Street, where the boot store had moved to a choice corner lot and the woman who sold handmade fabric had finally closed out and moved away. Out of town they drove, past the converted film-developing shack, now a drive-through for coffee in the morning, for people heading to work in Fresno. The fields and the orchards whizzed by, just as he remembered them, cyclical and permanent, and Highway 99 with its cars forever traveling. But Fresno itself, once his father chose an off-ramp for Olive Avenue, mystified him with its sudden vastness, its billboards for restaurants and stores located on what used to be the fringes of the northern part of the city. "Way over, on and on," his father said, waving his hand forward as if he knew why Emilio studied the signs. The deterioration of Olive Avenue, in the older part of Fresno, spoke everything about where the money was headed nowadays. Here were the cars with dangling mufflers and work trucks with bad paint jobs, the meat markets with their hand-painted signs in Spanish, the long-closed beauty salons with their broken neon signs, and everywhere people walking because they had no choice. On and on they went, Olive Avenue even more endless than Gold Street, the traffic surprisingly heavy and the red lights stopping them along the way. Finally, in one of the residential stretches between half-vacant strip malls, his father turned the car into a driveway lined with stacks and stacks of old, bald tires. The house was deep in the yard, hidden behind heavy shrubs, an old Chevy pickup parked at the end of the driveway. Immediately, Emilio saw the two high steps leading up to the porch. A bougainvillea trailed up the railing, but despite its deep, gorgeous color, it made Emilio think of the unruliness inside the house. How would he move around in a place like this, rooms and rooms of knickknacks and tiny tables, porcelain milkmaids and doilies, all leading back to the kitchen table, where he imagined the curandera would do her work? His father turned off the ignition and went to the front door, not turning to speak to Emilio. He knocked patiently on the screen door and waited, listening. When no immediate answer came, he opened the screen and knocked hard on the front door itself, and this time Emilio could sense the movement inside the house. The door opened and his father spoke his business, and after he closed his mouth, a woman poked her head out to look at the car. She seemed to study Emilio so intently that he finally waved at her, as if to assure her that he was real. The woman turned to Emilio's father and said something to him, which Emilio strained to hear, so he rolled down the window. After his father nodded in agreement, the woman stepped out. She was barefoot. Otherwise, she looked like any of the women you might see in Fresno wandering the aisles of the grocery store. Her black T-shirt was too long for her but still covered her prominent belly, and her faded blue jeans bulged at the thighs. Her lips bore a frosty shade of pink, and around each wrist she wore the bracelets that all the television commercials swore had healing powers, the ones with the tiny balls at each end, not quite meeting. The woman came over to the car, not bothering to say hello, and peeked in to get a look at Emilio's legs. She felt his forehead and ran her fingers under his chin as a doctor would. "Do you believe in God?" she asked him, and when Emilio did not immediately answer her, she said, "Well, do you?" Emilio told her that he guessed so. "That might be the problem," she said. "Do you believe in the devil?" This time, Emilio shook his head, and she felt his forehead one more time. "A lot of people do, you know. You should. He's the reason a lot of times." She went back to the front porch and walked past Emilio's father, who had removed his cowboy hat. They waited a few minutes, the bustle of Olive Avenue cut off enough by high shrubs to allow them to hear birds chattering in the branches, making a racket. A cat eased onto the porch and sniffed his father's boot so quietly that his father didn't notice. When he looked down and saw the cat, he gave it a shove with his foot, and the cat moved away but stared at him malevolently. The look on his father's face almost made Emilio laugh — the involuntary disgust his father always felt around animals clashing headlong with superstition. "It's just a cat," Emilio said, laughing, and it was the first time all day that he had been free of worry, of anguish. His father would not unlock his eyes from the cat, though, which sat on its haunches with tail twitching. Finally the woman came out and handed what looked like a Gerber baby-food jar to his father. Emilio heard her explaining the directions in Spanish, demonstrating with her hands how he was supposed to rub the salve, her hands circling as if she were washing a window. "¿Entiende?" she asked him, and when he nodded, her hand stopped cleaning the imaginary window and flattened out, expectant. His father took out his wallet and laid out bill after bill, so many that Emilio wondered if he hadn't planned long in advance to come to this curandera, the sudden tears only a show. After she counted the money, the woman folded the bills and reached deep into the black T-shirt to hide the bills in her bra, and then she walked back out to the car. "You rub that crema on you every night, you hear me?" she ordered, and put her hands on Emilio again, as if to feel once more whatever she might have felt before. "Someone put the evil eye on you," she told him as her hands traveled up the back of his neck and into the fringes of hair on the back of his head, rubbing him as a lover might, looking away from him in concentration, eyes closed. "You have to believe in it for it to go away." She lifted her hands and showed them to him, but Emilio saw nothing. "Feel them," she ordered, and he touched her palms, which had gone completely ice cold. "That's only the beginning," she said. "There's a lot more to take out of you."

Emilio and his father left the curandera's with the silence deeper between them, as if both had understood that the other would never understand. True enough, he had felt the woman's ice-cold palms, as if she had extracted something tangible, but the larger pain came in seeing his father count out bill after bill and lay them in the woman's hand, how she tucked them away, gone forever. What she said at the end of the visit, the way she stood looking at them as Emilio's father slowly backed out of the driveway and onto Olive Avenue, convinced Emilio that she would hold nothing but empty promises, visits extending as long as his father's wallet held out. He wanted to tell his father how foolish he was to believe in something like this. Even if it were true, how could anyone harness that kind of power in the service of cheating people? Olive Avenue stretched onward — they were traveling to the eastern end of Fresno instead of the highway, all the way down to Clovis Avenue with its tin-roof car washes and antiquated drive-ins, a busy road that edged south from the city into farmland and back out to the old Highway 99, the two-laner that sidled by the smaller towns of Fowler and Selma, for their trip home. Emilio could see the new 99 over to the west, the cars speeding along as always, never a moment's peace. He didn't ask his father why he had chosen this slower way home, but he guessed it had something to do with his father needing to come away from the curandera's with a sense of peace and calm, something heavy traffic would drain away from him. Here the speed limit was only fifty-five, and the offroads eased away in empty ribbons on either side, swallowed up by the grape vineyards. The old broken-windowed motels stood forlorn yet dignified. Emilio studied each of them as they passed by, thought of their histories, of the owners who had watched with worry as the new highway sprang up all those decades ago. What would a town like Fowler have become had the highway not come through? What would have happened instead had the highway not fated the town to move in another direction? To break the silence in the car, Emilio turned on the radio, not asking his father if he would mind, and he spent some time searching the dial until he found the station the mill foreman had played all through Shift Three. He caught the end of Freda Payne's "Band of Gold," and then a voice came over and urged them to shop downtown Selma — they would be passing through it in a matter of minutes. After some more ads, the announcer came on to answer a phone call, and the woman said she was from Caruthers. "Caruthers?" the announcer asked in mock surprise. "You get reception out there?" The woman laughed; she sounded older, her voice jagged, the kind of edge that comes from smoking and loving the wrong person. When the announcer asked her for her song dedication, she replied, " 'I'd Rather Go Blind,' but I don't remember who sang it. You remember?" she asked the announcer. "That would be Miss Etta James, darlin'," said the announcer immediately, as if he had known without having to look at anything, and the woman laughed again before she spoke the name of a man who lived in Laton. The announcer didn't ask for their story; he just played the song, and as Emilio listened, he watched the old motels go by, the used-car lots with their triangular plastic flags fluttering, the new strip malls and fast-food joints of Selma, just miles from home now. He listened to the song and thought of Catri, how she had stopped speaking to him after the accident and never visited him in the hospital. The story of how the accident happened must have gone around. Her parents were religious people, and she had been under their thumb for too long, on the edge of wounding them terribly by sneaking him into their house at night. Why the accident changed everything, Emilio didn't know. He had never been in love with her, but he had liked being with her, liked feeling under her blouse in the quiet of her bedroom at three in the morning, the way her hands would stroke his arms as if in disbelief at their size. He had never been in love with her, but he had whispered those words to her at four in the morning, her eyes glistening some in the dark with tears that never brimmed over. Emilio rested his head against the car door; another song came on, pitch perfect about loving and then not loving. Another song came, and then another, each one speaking to everything his head could contain about love, about Catri: heartbreak, second chances, the heartbreak of second chances. He thought of what the curandera had told him about belief, and he wondered if the same advice would count for Catri, if he willed it enough to happen. Momentarily, Emilio debated speaking aloud to his father, asking him if the curandera did love potions or spells, but he knew it would be the wrong question, and he felt ashamed at the thought of his father imagining him in his bedroom, pining after a girl long gone. But when they came back into town and turned onto Gold Street and he saw the front of Catri's house graced by the old Mercury her family had always owned, Emilio's heart skipped; but he refused the urge to turn his head for another look. He waited until they pulled up to their own house, for his father to get the wheelchair out of the trunk, and he gathered all his breath and strength to make the transition to the chair quick. He grabbed his father by the shoulders as he lifted, as if he could stand on his own. His father, stumbling a little in surprise, dropped him quickly into the chair, and Emilio immediately wheeled away from him. "I'll be back soon," he told his father. "¿Adónde vas?" his father asked, but Emilio kept going, maneuvering the chair despite the difficulty of the light gravel on their driveway. "Just down the street," he said, wheeling himself onto the road. "Thirty minutes." He would have to hug as close as possible to the cars parked on the side of the street: some of the houses still didn't have sidewalks in front, some had grass too thick for him to manage alone. But he moved down the road as fast as he could, spinning the wheels and ignoring the sudden tightness in his shoulders, his muscles balking. All those houses to pass, fifty-nine of them on this side. Neighborhood cars spotted him and waited patiently for him to get out of the way — cars he recognized, but he ignored the faces turning to look at him, waiting for him to say something first before greeting him. His head remained bent in determination. The street seemed strangely alive with neighbors, people looking up from the hoods of cars they were fixing, curtains parting, doors creaking open to get a better look at him passing—all people who knew his story, knew what had happened. Kids rode by on bicycles, staring at him as they passed, their weaving straightening out as if they suddenly knew why they must heed their parents' long-drawn calls to be safe. Emilio passed by the old house of the last white woman who had lived in their neighborhood—La Viejita, they had all called her, even though she didn't speak Spanish—a house with new occupants, but now lost to the elements: the overgrowth of weeds in the yard, a blackberry bush gone unruly and staining the sagging planks of what had once been a white picket fence. He had run away from home one foggy evening in winter, angry over a punishment meted out by his mother, and while his parents watched television, Emilio had tiptoed into the kitchen to steal one of the thick brown paper bags from United Market. In it he had put a pair of pants and his two favorite shirts, careful to tuck a pair of socks and underwear at the bottom in case the bag tipped over and spilled everything out. He had left quietly through the back door, crept along the side of the house, and walked down Gold Street, the whole length of it, aiming for the railroad tracks a few blocks beyond there. Sometime during the night, he imagined, a train would pull slowly along the rails, and he would jump into an open boxcar and it would take him far, far away. But when the stop sign at the end of Gold Street came into view, barely visible through the thickening fog, the warm lamplight in a window of La Viejita's house had urged him to go and knock on the door. When she opened it, he told her without hesitation that he had run away from home. "Pray to the Lord Jesus," La Viejita told him while he looked past her into the house, at the clarity of its white walls, the lamps on little tables, a delicious scent of something cooking, something he had never smelled at home. "Jesus will take care of you," she assured him, closing the door slowly, inch by inch. "Now go on back home." Left alone in the austerity of the fog, he became frightened, and he quickly walked back home, clutching his grocery bag of clothes. La Viejita's house had no such look of warmth now that she didn't live there. One of the windows sat open, and a curtain with an ugly yellow and brown pattern curled a lip of itself at a slight breeze. The front yard, once green and lush, had surrendered to dust, and the formidable oak tree had been pruned down to nubs, scars around the trunk where a dog had been chained. Emilio moved on just a few houses more to Catri's place, which wasn't in much better condition than La Viejita's. He stopped at the edge of the front yard, unable to go any farther because of the height of the grass, the heavy gravel in their driveway. Lifting an arm, he waved futilely at the window as if someone were staring out at him, and just when he put his arm down because of how foolish he felt, the door cracked open. A woman's head popped out — Catri's mother, who squinted at him in recognition — and when she popped her head back in, she left the door open. A moment later, Catri came out of the house, arms folded shyly across her breasts as if it were the cool, foggy evening Emilio had run away, and she walked toward him across the grass. She wasn't smiling. "Catri," he called out to her. "Hi. How are you?" Emilio asked, wanting to see her smile. She had filled out in the hips, and the way she crossed her arms made them look plumper than they might have been. But she was still pretty and she still had the look in her eyes of expecting a good love from someone. "I'm married," she told him, even before she reached the street. "I'm married now and I have a baby." Her crossed arms took on a posture of both defensiveness and shame, as if she now had to confront the truth of never having visited him in the hospital. Behind her, he could see the curtains moving in the windows. If her husband had been there, he would surely have walked out by now. But even without that threat, Emilio put his hands on the wheels and slowly turned himself around, not bothering to look at her. He thought he heard the shuffle of her sandals coming after him, but he kept moving himself forward, leaving all the questions behind. Why? Who? When? Why not? How come? There was no rush to his movement and no deliberate slowing, just turn after turn of the wheels, the rubber working against the calluses made long ago on his palms. All those years ago, returning from La Viejita's, he had bolted into the front door to the surprise of his parents, and it had been his father who opened his arms to him, put away the clothes in the grocery bag, and gave him a cup of Mexican hot chocolate to put him to sleep. It would be his father now, much older, whom he would see once he reached their house, pausing at the lip of the ramp to be led inside. Yet it still surprised Emilio somewhat when, house in sight, he saw his father sitting on the ramp with his cowboy hat in hand, waiting patiently. His father walked out into the street without asking if he needed help, and he pushed Emilio the rest of the way into the yard and up the ramp, then wheeled Emilio into his room, all without saying a word.

It was nearly four in the afternoon now and his stomach growled, but he couldn't ask his father for food. The Gerber jar of crema was on his nightstand, conspicuous, as if it were a jewel resting on a pillow. Emilio stared at it for a moment, but not even a pinprick of curiosity seized him. He folded down one of the chair's armrests and willed himself over to the bed, surprised how his hurt allowed him to move so determinedly. The urge to cry overwhelmed him. He had not cried in all this time, all these hours alone. His body had felt like one of the wells over in the plum orchards, deep and mysterious and dark, but soundless when you dropped something into it. The house was quiet and he stifled his crying as best he could, but the tears kept streaming. He kept crying, circles and circles of grief edging outward, until he noticed the light in his room had changed. It was nowhere near evening, but there was enough fading sunlight to remind him how long he had been weeping, how exhausted he had made himself. Emilio wanted sleep now, and he probed his secret stash for a couple of pills, tucking them under his tongue, willing some saliva to wash them down. A few moments later, he reached again and took two more. Then two more, remembering break time on Shift Three, one more shot of whiskey, one more hit on the joint. Not knowing if he had crossed the line until he actually crossed it. He lay in the gradually disappearing light and drifted off into dream, the rustle of the grape vineyards during those break times, the dark shadows of the men hoarding their own stashes. Emilio broke through those vineyards to a warm white house with yellow light in the windows, and he approached, opening the door without knocking, and there at a simple brown table he found himself, wearing his deep green football jersey. He rose in greeting. "Emilio," he said to himself. "It's good to see you up and around." It filled him with a flood of joy to hear that, to feel his own hand in his, a hand of understanding, of reconciliation, of appeasement, of sorrow and redemption, of love. He shook hands vigorously, in awe of seeing himself standing once more, not wanting to let go — he felt his heart break, knowing he would have to. His father woke him, and when Emilio opened his eyes, the light of day in the room had been replaced by the glow of a lamp. It was late, but there was no telling how late. His father felt his forehead, slick with perspiration, then helped him with a bedpan as if he knew he was filled to bursting and wouldn't make it to the bathroom. When Emilio was done, his father wordlessly set the bedpan on the floor and helped him remove his pants, leaving Emilio in his boxers. He took the Gerber jar of crema and opened it. Even before he swirled it onto his fingers, Emilio could smell it — a mixture of lard, oranges, something peppery. He watched as his father smoothed the crema onto his thin legs, white and nearly hairless, working the mixture over his knees all the way down to his ankles, over the ugly scars. His father used more and more of it, not being thrifty with it as they had been with everything else in life, rubbing hard with belief, and Emilio kept watching, his eyes focused on the broken promise of his father's wedding band. The clock said it was past five in the morning. Emilio thought of the pills again. Finally, when his father was finished, he put the little jar down on the nightstand and covered Emilio with a blanket. "Buenas noches, m'ijo," he said, and reached down for the bedpan as he left the room, turning off the light. For a long time, Emilio lay in the dark. He thought of Catri. He thought of her baby and her husband. He thought of his father. He thought of his mother. He thought of the pills and their answers, and he remembered the taste of whiskey. He thought of La Viejita, and he thought of God and the devil and which of them she might know. He thought of love and not having it, of who had it and who got to keep it. He raised his arms in the dark, stretched them, willing, and when he brought them down, his hand bumped against the little jar of crema on the nightstand. Emilio opened it and smelled — the lard, the oranges, the pepper. Some violet from the coming dawn filtered through the window. He took the little bit of crema that was left in the jar and worked it onto the calluses on each of his palms, a long moment of circling his fingers in the dark violet of early morning, and when he was done, they felt smooth and absolutely brand-new.

GRACIAS

I WISH TO THANK each of the editors of the following publications, who published earlier versions of these stories with such kind enthusiasm: *Epoch* ("Lindo y Querido" and "Tell Him About Brother John"), *Glimmer Train Stories* ("Bring Brang Brung"), *Rush Hour* ("The Heart Finds Its Own Conclusion"), and *Swink* ("The Comeuppance of Lupe Rivera"). My deep appreciation always to the good people of Northwestern University Press, who published my first book, and who continue to receive me with open arms. Gracias to the National Endowment for the Arts for bringing me to grateful tears by awarding me a literature fellowship.

Several people bear special mention: Stuart Bernstein, agent and faith healer, is always ready with needed encouragement and belief. El querido Chuck Adams, my editor at Algonquin Books, treated the lives of these characters as if they were Real (because he knows they are). Helena María Viramontes, mentor and literary madrina, is on every page here and those still to come. Abrazos over the many miles to mi familia, who now know why writing is so important to me and understand why I am so far away. Amá, gracias por las llamadas cada domingo—toditas, toditas.

Finally, I want to thank the good friends who stood by me during the difficult time when these stories were written, who knew when to ask if I wanted to sit out on the front steps and just think aloud, talk some: I will let them name themselves.

ABOUT THE AUTHOR

Manuel Muñoz is the author of *Zigzagger,* a short story collection. He is the recipient of a Constance Saltonstall Foundation Individual Artist's Grant in Fiction and a National Endowment for the Arts literature fellowship. His work has appeared in many journals, including *Rush Hour, Swink, Epoch, Glimmer Train,* and *Boston Review,* and has aired on NPR's *Selected Shorts.* A native of Dinuba, California, Manuel graduated from Harvard University and received his MFA in creative writing at Cornell University. He now lives in New York City.